Mo
Tha
for r
♡ Sheri Abild

A Sunny Day
In Winter

Sheri Abild

Copyright © 2023 by Sheri Abild

Published by Sunny Love Stories LLC

All rights reserved.

No part of this publication may be reproduced, distributed, or transmitted in any form or by any means, including photocopying, recording, or other electronic or mechanical methods, without the prior written permission of the publisher, except as permitted by U.S. copyright law. For permission requests, please contact the author at sunnylovestories@gmail.com

This story is a work of fiction, based loosely on the author's life.

ISBN: 978-1-960181-00-8 (paperback)

ISBN: 978-1-960181-01-5 (e-book)

♥

This story is dedicated to my husband Brandon,
the real-life Brayden, and the best thing
that has ever happened to me.

And to my cat Sidney Michaela,
the real-life Ellie, and my furry co-author.

Chapter 1

♥

I woke up at 6 a.m. to the sound of my phone ringing. I looked at the screen and smiled when I saw it was my parents.

"Good morning," I answered cheerfully.

"Happy birthday to you! Happy birthday to you! Happy birthday dear Sunny, happy birthday to you!" They sang together.

"Thanks, Mom. Thanks, Dad," I said as I sat up in bed. I always look forward to their birthday morning phone call and off-key singing.

"We wanted to call you nice and early before Allison shows up," my mom said. "What time are you heading to Chester?"

"In a little more than an hour. The Winter Carnival starts at ten, and we want to stop by a local bakery that gets glowing reviews first. I hear they make an awesome chocolate cake with chocolate frosting!"

Every year I celebrate my birthday with my two favorite things—lasagna and chocolate cake with chocolate frosting. I went to my parent's house last night, and my mom made her famous lasagna, knowing that Allison and I would be out for the day today.

"Are you guys sure you don't want to come with us?" I asked, worried that they might be feeling left out.

"No, Sunny, that's okay," my dad replied. "You know the cold bothers my hips now."

"Enjoy your cake and tell Allison and the kids we said hi." I could hear the smile in my mom's voice.

"I love you guys," I said, feeling happy that my day had started with their singing. "Thanks for calling and singing to me."

"You're welcome, Sunny," my dad said.

"We love you too," my mom chimed in. "Have fun."

I got up out of bed and went to the kitchen for some coffee and gave morning treats to my gray tabby cat, Ellie—short for Elephant. I was just about to get in the shower when my phone rang again. This time it was Allison, my best friend since the third grade.

"Good morning, beautiful! Are you and the kids excited for the carnival?"

"Happy birthday, pretty lady." She tried to sound cheerful, but I sensed some hesitation in her voice.

"Thanks. Is everything okay?"

"I'm really sorry, but Zachary woke up with a stomach ache this morning. We're all so disappointed. Everyone was looking forward to a fun day."

2

A SUNNY DAY IN WINTER

My heart sank at hearing her news. I could tell from her voice that she felt terrible. But it wasn't her fault, and I didn't want her to feel guilty. So, I smiled and said—as cheerfully as possible, "It's okay, maybe we can go next year. Besides, I have some tv shows to catch up on. I'll just hang out here with Ellie today."

"No, you will not! You are not going to sit at home and watch tv with your cat on your birthday!"

I was quiet for a moment, caught off guard by her sternness, although I should be used to it by now.

I think she was afraid she hurt my feelings because her voice was softer when she spoke again. "I'm sorry Sunny. I just don't want to see you waste your birthday sitting around your apartment. You've been looking forward to this for weeks, and you actually have a Saturday off from work. At least go and check out that bakery. You deserve to have your favorite cake on your birthday. And those reviews weren't just raving about the food—they also said that the people there are lovely and welcoming."

"I guess I could go by myself," I said quietly, with a bit of apprehension.

"You can do this, Sunny—you're the friendly one," she said encouragingly. "Your self-confidence has come a long way over the past two years, and I know how hard you've worked to get over everything."

"Thanks, Allison. I know."

She was right. I've been excited about the Winter Carnival since I saw a flyer at the grocery store. There's no use in sitting around all day when I could be out meeting new people. And at the very least, I could sit quietly in the bakery and enjoy my birthday cake. And she has a point about my self-confidence. I've made so much progress over the last couple of years, and doing something alone could be a good way of getting out of my comfort zone.

"Besides, the weather forecast is looking rather cloudy for today, and I think Chester could use some of the sunshine that always seems to follow you."

"You're right," I said, a wave of confidence flooding me. "I'm going to Chester, and I will have a great birthday no matter what! Tell Zachary I hope he feels better."

"Thanks, I will," she replied. "And Sunny, I'm really proud of you."

AN HOUR LATER, DRESSED in jeans and a yellow sweater, I was ready to head out the door. I had put a few loose curls in my long, dark brown hair, and my makeup was light and natural—just enough to accentuate my brown eyes against my fair complexion.

I paired my favorite pink, and white plaid scarf with my ivory wool coat adorned with pretty buttons and a tapered waist. Pink is my favorite color, and my sweater's cheerful yellow shade reminds me of the sunshine, so it was my perfect birthday outfit. I put on my fur-lined black boots and grabbed my mittens made of upcycled pink sweaters. We native Vermonters know how to dress for a day out in the cold.

I patted Ellie on the head as I went out the door, and she gave me an encouraging meow. I was determined to enjoy my birthday—even if my plans had changed a little. It's about thirty minutes to Chester, a quaint little Vermont town. Every year they put on their Winter Carnival, and every year I wanted to go. The flyers they put up to promote the event made it look fun and welcoming—with things like sledding, a snowman contest, and vendors selling food and crafts.

I turned off my street and smiled as I drove by Allen Brother's Store on the right side of Route 5. Their trademark large red apple identifies them, and it cheers me whenever I see it. The main reason why I love the place is my grandfather. He stops there every morning for a coffee and donut, and sometimes I join him to chat about the happenings at the local Fire Department.

I got on Interstate 91 at Exit 5 and took it up north about ten miles, getting off at the Rockingham Exit. I turned left off the exit ramp onto Route 103, heading toward Chester—enjoying the beautiful scenery on my way. It had snowed yesterday, and a blanket of crisp whiteness covered the bare tree branches. Vermont is well-known for its vibrant fall foliage, and winter can be just as stunning after a fresh snowfall.

A few miles down 103, I passed by the Vermont Country Store—a large, rustic building with a sprawling front porch. It's a well-known stop in our area, attracting tourists from all over. I smiled when I noticed my favorite detail of the Rockingham property—the *Kissing Bridge*—a small covered bridge that sets a very romantic mood for couples in love.

As I approached downtown Chester, I turned left down a side street where signs were directing me for parking. A gentleman wearing a yellow reflective vest labeled *Volunteer* pointed me to a plowed-out open field. He requested a five-dollar donation, explaining that the parking proceeds would benefit the local humane society. A feeling of warmth spread through me as I paid him, knowing that I would be helping animals in need—animals like my Ellie, whom I found as a kitten on the side of the road.

I walked the short distance back to Main Street, excitement bubbling inside me as I approached a winter wonderland. I stared all around with childlike wonder—everything looking so magical, so quintessential Vermont. Strings of holiday lights cheered up the plain brown light poles lining each side of the street, shimmering in the early morning fog. Winter decorations adorned the windows and storefronts of many shops and cafes—a welcome sight to celebrate the season. White, freshly fallen snow along the roadside gave a bright, sparkling contrast to the black asphalt of the pavement. A large, vibrant banner announcing the Winter Carnival spanned the width of the street overhead, welcoming all attendees from near and far.

Many local vendors and crafters were bustling around outside, putting the final touches on their displays. Ladies under a pop-up tent showed off their knitted hats, scarves, and mittens. The tent next to them displayed lotion and lip balm for sale—all appropriate for a winter day. As I walked around, I noticed that the sun was starting to peek out from behind the clouds, and I could hear the vendors chatting amongst themselves about the welcome change in weather.

The next tent had urns—labeled *Regular, Decaf,* and *Hot Water*—and was occupied by a tall man in a blue coat with short, dirty blond hair. I watched from afar as he arranged display cases for various pastries. The pink and white striped banner hanging up at the back of his tent had whimsical blue lettering that read:

Something Sweet Bakery
On The Green, Chester, Vermont

That's the bakery Allison and I had read great things about—and I knew I had to find it.

I looked over the Chester Green—a sizeable oval patch of snow-covered ground about 450 feet long. Several maple and elm trees towered against the sky, with holiday lights wrapped around their trunks—making them look even more majestic. A few park benches and picnic tables were scattered amongst the trees, and the focal point of the whole area was a small white gazebo—the perfect size for the couple sitting inside to enjoy an intimate moment in the fresh air. Icicles hanging from the snow-covered roof glistened in the morning sunshine, adding to the romantic atmosphere. I admired the glorious view for a minute, then I pulled my phone from my coat pocket and took a few pictures—needing to capture the winter charm that can only be found in small-town New England.

A long row of storefronts sat just beyond The Green, separated by a one-lane strip of pavement. I scanned the row of shops and noticed a bookstore, a quilting shop, and a classic Victorian bed and breakfast—painted a calming pale yellow, offset with exquisite purple shutters. Next to the bed and breakfast was a red brick building with pink and white striped awnings over the windows and a sign above the door that read:

Something Sweet Bakery

A huge smile spread across my face as I headed eagerly toward the door—excited to see what awaited me on the other side.

Chapter 2

♥

I OPENED THE DOOR to the bakery and stepped inside. The place was even more delightful than I had envisioned, and I closed my eyes and breathed in the sweet aromas of cinnamon and nutmeg. Fresh cinnamon rolls and coffee were the first things I noticed, and I felt instantly energized. Then, I opened my eyes and took in the beautiful sight, the bakery looking just as sweet as it smelled. Several tables were beautifully arranged throughout the room—all with crisp, white tablecloths, a vase holding pink and white carnations, and white wooden chairs with pink cushions. Fairy lights attached to the ceiling twinkled overhead, and my heart swelled as I daydreamed about the romantic mood they would set in dimmer lighting. I imagined the sheer pink curtains flowing in a gentle breeze on warm days as I took in the ivory walls decorated with several photos encased in maple frames. Three large chalkboards hung on the wall upfront, and someone with artistic handwriting carefully wrote out the

9

menu—with food listed on the left and drinks on the right. My joy grew as I read the one in the middle:

Welcome to our family bakery!
Where the answer is always "Something Sweet!"

Maple flooring and a majestic, live edge maple counter offset the pink and white—a unique way to pull the whole place together.

I stepped up to the counter and was greeted by a friendly face. A lady in her late fifties with short brown hair and brown eyes wore a gray sweater underneath a pink and white striped apron, with the words *Something Sweet Bakery* written in the same whimsical blue lettering as the sign.

"Good morning," she greeted me with a cheerful smile. "I'm Lauren. Welcome to our family bakery."

"Thanks, Lauren." I returned her smile. "I'm Sunny."

Just then, the kitchen door swung open, and in walked a young woman carrying a tray of muffins. She had the same shade of brown hair tied up in a messy ponytail and brown eyes, and I guessed her to be Lauren's daughter. She was wearing a matching apron but with a light blue sweater underneath. My assumption was correct when Lauren said, "Sunny, this is my daughter April."

"Hi, April," I said to her.

She set down her tray, smiled at me, and said, "Hi, Sunny, it's nice to meet you."

"Your bakery is beautiful," I complimented them, looking around. "It's so warm and cozy in here, and it feels like home."

"Thanks, that's just what we were going for," April replied. "What can we get for you?"

I scanned the offerings inside the pastry cabinet—orange scones, bear claws, and blueberry muffins all caught my eye. However, my smile fell when I saw the chocolate cake with chocolate frosting sign and noticed the empty space. I think the two ladies sensed my disappointment because April said, "There's a fresh cake in the oven right now. We put the desserts out at lunchtime."

I let out a sigh of relief. "Great, that's my favorite." The two of them shared a look, and I felt I was missing out on a joke. "What?" I asked.

"That's my brother's favorite, too. He owns the bakery with me," April explained.

"Oh, so you ladies don't own it together?"

"Mom helps out all the time, but Brayden and I are the owners. My brother is a real saint for letting me girly up the place with all the pink and white flowers and table settings everywhere," she said with a laugh. "But since I'm the one out front greeting the customers, he encouraged me to set everything up how I wanted it. He says I'm the face of the business, and he's just the numbers guy. But the truth is, he's way more than just the numbers guy to this place."

"Well, as you can see"—I took a step back and gestured to my coat and scarf—"I'm a big fan of pink and white myself."

"My granddaughter would love your scarf. She's just as girly as her mom here," Lauren said, putting her arm around April's shoulders. "And based on the looks of you and your outfit, you're going to fit in really well around here."

I couldn't help but smile. In just these first few minutes, I felt right at home—like I already belong.

Watching Lauren and April together, I thought it was beautiful how they all took part in the bakery—a true family operation. Looking around, though, I could see what April meant. Her brother must be quite the guy to let her have so much creative control and 'girly up the place,' as she put it.

"So, what can we get for you in the meantime, Sunny?" April asked me.

I looked back inside the cabinet again. "I will take a cinnamon roll and a coffee, please. And I'll make sure to try the cake later."

April put my cinnamon roll on a plate while Lauren poured me a cup of coffee. After I paid them, I took my treats to a table nestled in the corner, draping my coat and scarf over my chair. I sat down and took my first bite of the cinnamon roll. Wow! Was it amazing! It had the perfect balance of cinnamon and sugar, and the cream cheese frosting on top had just the right amount of sweetness.

A SUNNY DAY IN WINTER

My table was next to a window overlooking The Green, and I took in the sights happening outside the bakery as I enjoyed my breakfast. A couple strolled by, walking hand in hand, and I could hear their two kids excitedly telling them about the fun they planned to have today. Over on The Green, an older couple who had just left the bakery went up to one of the benches. He brushed off the snow, and they sat down, enjoying the sunshine and sipping their coffees. I smiled as a young couple walked past the window, pushing a stroller. They looked affectionately at their tiny baby—a sweet young family out for a morning walk.

Even though I was alone, I didn't feel lonely here. My birthday was off to a great start, after all.

I WAS ENJOYING MY cinnamon roll, coffee, and the sights outside so much that I had tuned out everything happening inside the bakery—until I heard a voice next to me.

"Everyone looks so happy, don't they?"

It was Lauren. She sat across from me and smiled as she looked out the window to see a young lady about April's age walking by with a little girl.

"They do," I agreed. "Chester looks like such a tight-knit community."

"Are you watching for some friends to show up?"

"Actually, I'm here by myself today. My best friend and her family were supposed to come with me, but her son woke up sick this morning. I thought about just staying home, but she encouraged me to come anyway." I paused for a moment and added, "And I'm glad I did. You and April have been so friendly. It's like I'm not even by myself."

Her face lit up as she reached across the table and squeezed my hand. "Thanks, Sunny. I'm glad to hear you feel welcome with us."

April walked up with a pot of coffee in her hand. "Would you like a refill, Sunny?"

"Yes, please."

"You seem to have brought the sunshine to Chester with you today," she remarked as she topped off my mug and looked out the window.

"I've always had that effect on the weather," I said, smiling.

"April, Sunny's here by herself today," Lauren said to her daughter. "Her best friend was supposed to come with her, but she had to cancel because her son is sick."

"Well, we can't have you spend the day alone." April thought for a moment, then said, "My kids still need another person on their team for the snowman competition. Why don't you join them?"

"Really?" I asked, touched by her kind invitation.

"Yeah, I'm sure they would love to have you help them. Like my mom said, my daughter is super girly, so I know the two of you would get along great."

"Now we have to get your brother out here," Lauren said, looking at April. "The hardest part is getting him away from that computer of his. But, if we can do that, there's no way he'll be able to say no."

"Give me your phone." April held her hand out to her mom. "I'll text him from your phone. If I do it from mine, he'll accuse me of being a bossy pants."

I laughed as Lauren put her hand to the side of her mouth and said, "Which she kind of is."

"Yeah, but I don't need him telling me that," April said, laughing as well. Then, after she sent the text, she handed her mom's phone back to her. "I even worded it like you would have."

Lauren looked at what April had typed and smiled. "That sounds just like me!"

I could see April still thinking as she turned to me. "My husband is outside under the bakery's tent, putting the final touches on setting everything up. I still have a few things to bring out to him. Would you mind helping me, Sunny?"

"Not at all," I replied, happy to feel like a part of their group.

Then she shifted her focus to her mom. "The kids are in the kitchen decorating cookies right now. After Marissa gets here, bring them outside and tell them to lay it on extra-thick when Brayden shows up, especially Cassidy." She turned to me and said, "My daughter is the one person my brother cannot say no to. Once he's out there,

Mr. Serious himself won't be able to back out on the snowman competition."

"Speaking of the kids," Lauren said, standing up, "I should go check on them and see what kind of a mess they're making. I'll see you two outside soon."

After she had left, April said to me, "I'll go grab the last couple of items that we need under the tent. Thanks for agreeing to help my kids, Sunny. They'll be so excited to meet you."

"Thanks for inviting me, April," I said with a big smile. "I can't wait to meet my team members."

The online reviews were correct—the food here is excellent, and the people are amiable. Could this day possibly get any better?

Chapter 3

♥

I PUT ON MY coat, scarf, and mittens and followed April outside to the tent that her family had set up. She was carrying stacks of napkins and paper plates, and she had given me a package of paper cups. There was now coffee and hot water in the urns and pastries in the display cases.

"Sunny, this is my husband, Sam," April said to me as we set down everything we were carrying.

"It's nice to meet you, Sunny," he said, shaking my hand.

"You too," I replied with a smile.

"I have the best job out of everyone around here"—he patted his stomach—"I am the bakery's official taste tester."

I gave a little laugh. "Now that's a job my dad could get on board with."

"Sunny's going to be the fourth team member for Kyle and Cassidy at the snowman competition."

Sam's hazel eyes grew wide with disbelief as he looked at his wife. "So, you got Mr. Serious to step away from his computer?"

"Mom and I are working on that," she said with a devious grin.

"I don't know about you two." He laughed and shook his head good-naturedly. "And speaking of the snowman competition"—he checked his watch—"I should get heading over there and see what they still need help with." He kissed April on his way out of the tent. "Good luck to your brother. He's going to need it."

April picked up the coffee cups and handed them to me, leading me behind the table with the pastries on it. "Would you mind stacking these up on the table next to you?"

"Sure."

I didn't get very far before realizing I needed more dexterity, so I pulled off my mittens and stuffed them into my coat pockets. As I stacked the cups, April was busy arranging the pastries in the display case. After I got done, I looked up to see Lauren coming under the tent with two excited kids in tow. First was a boy about seven or eight years old, with brown hair and eyes, wearing a green snowsuit with mittens dangling from his sleeves. He was followed by a girl of about five or six with dirty blonde hair and blue eyes, wearing a hot pink snowsuit, hat, and mittens. *She's my kind of girl*, I thought.

"Sunny, these are my kids, Kyle and Cassidy."

"Hi Kyle, hi Cassidy," I said to them with a friendly smile.

"Hi," Kyle replied quietly.

Cassidy was looking at my outfit. "I like your scarf. It's pretty. Pink is my favorite color."

"Thanks, Cassidy. Pink is my favorite color too."

"What did I tell you?" Lauren said as she stepped around to the back of the table with April and me.

Suddenly, the kids ran out of the tent, yelling excitedly, "Uncle Brayden!" They ran up and hugged a man coming down the sidewalk, then followed behind him as he entered the tent.

"Here are the cups you wanted, Mom," he said as he handed Lauren a package of paper coffee cups. "Although it looks like you don't need them."

"Well, I needed a way to get you out here—all you do is work. So, I figured if I made up something about the bakery, it would get you away from that computer of yours."

He lifted his sunglasses to the top of his head—and I was met with a pair of the most brilliant blue eyes I had ever seen. I felt an instant connection to him—something I have never felt before. Time seemed to stop at that moment, and I wondered if he felt it too.

"Brayden, this is Sunny," April said to him. "She's going to help you and the kids build a snowman for the competition."

He didn't say anything. Neither one of us did. My heart was pounding, and I found myself suddenly unable to speak—which was very unusual for me. All I could do was stare at him—my eyes fixed on his. I really couldn't tell you what color his hair was or what he was wearing—that's how much of an effect he was having on me. His eyes were locked on mine—holding me there—making me unable to move. Not that I wanted to. Even in these first few seconds with him, I felt like I belonged in his presence—and he kept drawing me in further.

Lauren gently moved me out of the way to set down the package of cups she was holding. That was enough to break me out of my trance, and I blurted out, "I have a cat named Elephant," in a voice that sounded like a squeaky chicken. I instantly flushed with embarrassment and nervously ran my hand through my hair. Unfortunately, my fingers got tangled, and after tugging them free, my arm bumped right into the cups I had just stacked up—toppling them all over. *Nice Sunny*, I thought, *what a way to make a first impression*. Good thing Allison's not here. She's always getting after me to not lead with my cat when talking to an attractive man. I really do need to start listening to her. After quickly restacking the cups, I took a deep, steadying breath and looked back at Brayden. His face was lit up with a huge smile, and I felt myself blush all over again.

Luckily, my embarrassing moment was cut short by Kyle. "Uncle Brayden, you have to come build a snowman with us."

I let out a sigh of relief as Cassidy chimed in, "Please, Uncle Brayden. You're the best at building snowmen.

We'll win the contest for sure if you help us!" She looked up at him with pleading eyes, and I thought, *Oh, she's good*.

From the look on his face, he knew there was no getting out of it. "You can't possibly say no to that," April said as she pushed her brother out of the tent. "And don't forget Sunny." She grabbed me by the arm and gave me a gentle shove in his direction—and I found myself out on the sidewalk.

THE KIDS RAN AHEAD, leaving Brayden and me to walk together—just the two of us. Now that I was no longer under the spell of his eyes, I was able to take in the rest of his appearance. He was around my age, with dark brown hair—a few flecks of gray interspersed—and about four or five inches taller than me. He was wearing dark wash, slim-fit jeans, and brown boots, and he looked so sharp in his black wool coat, a red and black plaid scarf visible above the top button. His clean-shaven face was classically handsome, like an old-time movie star.

As we walked, he said, "So, a cat named Elephant, huh?"

"It was my dad's suggestion. She's a gray tiger," I replied, my voice sounding much more normal now. "We call her Ellie for—" I cut myself off—Allison's voice screaming at me inside my head to *Shut up!*

He smiled at me, and I felt myself relax. "You have a very pretty voice."

"Thank you," I said, grateful that he noticed.

"Is this your first time coming to the Winter Carnival?"

"It is, but I've wanted to come and check it out for years. I was supposed to come today with friends, but they had to cancel at the last minute. So, when I told your mom and sister that I was here by myself, they invited me to join you and the kids for the snowman competition."

"I'm glad they did." He looked at me for a long moment. "So, you're from the area?"

"I grew up one exit down the Interstate in Westminister."

"You even say it like a local," he laughed.

"I was in the fifth grade before I realized there's not an extra 'i' in my hometown's name, but that's how I always heard it growing up," I said, laughing as well. I love that little quirk about my hometown. It's something unique to us.

"Does your family still live in Westminister?" He grinned at me as he pronounced it the locals' way.

"They do. In fact, my grandfather just celebrated his fiftieth anniversary with the Volunteer Fire Department." I smiled as I thought of my grandfather and his pride in serving our community.

"Wow! Fifty years—that's incredible," he replied, genuinely impressed.

"Yeah, he's always been the type to help his fellow man. It's one of the things I love most about him."

"Well, he sounds like a great man."

"Thanks, Brayden, he really is," I said, reaching up and touching his arm.

As soon as my hand landed on him, I stopped—once again held in my tracks by the presence of this man. He stopped as well—patiently waiting while I stared at the bare skin of my thumb, ever so slightly brushing the soft wool of his coat. It felt so natural, so right to be touching him, and I wondered how he felt about it. I shifted my gaze to read his expression and noticed he wasn't looking at my hand. Instead, he was looking at my face—his eyes sparkling with amusement as he watched me.

"So," I said, dropping my hand as we started walking again. "Did you grow up around here?"

"Right here in Chester."

I pulled my mittens out of my coat pockets, and as I fumbled to get them back on, I glanced up to see him watching me. His huge smile once again returned, like how he looked when I told him about Ellie.

Get a grip, Sunny! I heard Allison's voice scolding me again. *What is wrong with you? First, you squeak at him about Ellie, and now you can't even get your mittens back on? This guy is going to think you are completely crazy!* I took another deep, steadying breath and calmly finished putting my mittens back on, thinking about something else I could ask him.

"How long has your family owned the bakery?"

"A few years," he answered.

23

"It's not just the Winter Carnival that brought me to town. Your family's bakery did too."

"Oh yeah?" he asked curiously.

"I read some reviews online that your chocolate cake with chocolate frosting is the best around. It's my favorite. I have it every year for my birthday."

Before he could say anything else, we were interrupted by two impatient kids.

"Uncle Brayden, Sunny, the snowman contest is about ready to start," Kyle said urgently.

"Come on." Cassidy tugged on her uncle's hand. "We don't want them to start without us."

"Well, let's go then," I said, smiling at Brayden. "I hear we have an expert snowman builder on our team."

We picked up our pace, and the three of us listened as Cassidy chatted up a storm about the snowman she was going to make.

Chapter 4

♥

We arrived at Cobleigh Field a few minutes later, and I felt much more comfortable and like myself again. The awkward, crazy cat lady fumbling with her mittens had thankfully disappeared—replaced by my typically friendly, outgoing, and cheerful personality. A large crowd gathered to watch the competition, and we joined the line at the registration table, with several groups of four people waiting in front of us.

"Brayden! It's so good to see you here," the woman standing in front of us said as she reached up and hugged him. A short lady in her fifties with mid-length blonde hair and wire-rimmed glasses was standing next to a taller gentleman of the same age with dark hair and sunglasses. They looked like such a sweet couple—reminding me of my parents as I watched them holding hands in matching blue winter coats. They had two children with them—a boy and a girl, both with brown hair and eyes, and they looked to be about the same age as Kyle and Cassidy.

They wore snowsuits and mittens covered in snow, so I figured they had already been enjoying some winter fun this morning.

"Hi Danielle," he said to her. "Is Rebecca watching the inn?"

"She is. She sent Patrick and me out here with the kids while she cleans up after breakfast. But that's okay. Building a snowman with our grandkids sounds like a lot more fun than doing dishes," she answered with a cheerful laugh. Then, she looked at Kyle and Cassidy and said, "It looks like you've been roped in by a couple of kids yourself."

"Yeah, these two have been going on and on about building a snowman together ever since my sister told them that we won the competition three years in a row when we were kids." He smiled as he looked at Cassidy, still holding his hand, and said, "This one here knows I can't say no to her." Then he turned to look at me and said, "Sunny, this is Patrick and Danielle. They own the inn next door to the bakery."

"It's nice to meet you, Sunny," Danielle said. "These are our grandkids, Annie and Liam."

"It's nice to meet you too," I replied, looking at their happy faces.

"The weather cleared up so nicely this morning," Patrick observed. "It's good to see the sun shining."

"It feels great to be out in the fresh air instead of cooped up inside working. But look who I'm talking to," Danielle said, playfully nudging Brayden with her elbow. He just nodded in agreement.

After they had registered, Brayden and I stepped up to the table with the kids.

"Will wonders never cease," the middle-aged woman sitting behind the table said in a spirited voice. She lifted her sunglasses to reveal beautiful green eyes, surrounded by heavy, black eyeliner and mascara. She set her sunglasses on top of her burgundy hair and said with a playful grin, "If it's not Brayden Montgomery in the flesh—out actually having some fun for once." Wow, somebody else was surprised to see him.

"Hi, Vicki," he replied politely, but it looked like he was trying to avoid making eye contact with her. I'm guessing her eyes scanning him up and down were making him a little uncomfortable. "My mom concocted a scheme to get me out here. Something about how I work too much and wanting to get me away from my computer." He looked at me and smiled. "But it's okay. This time I don't mind."

Vicki looked at him with a curious expression, like she was trying to read his face, then said, "Okay. So, we have Kyle and Cassidy Fournier." She was writing their names as she spoke. "Brayden Montgomery, and—" She stopped and looked at me—realizing she didn't know me. "A newcomer."

"Sunny Jackson," I said to her.

"Well, Sunny Jackson, you picked a great guy to be on a team with." She looked back at Brayden, and as her eyes scanned him again, she said, "And looking extra handsome today if I may say so myself. You look even younger when you shave." After she got done giving him the once over, she asked us, "What would you like your team name to be?"

"Something Sweet Bakery—if that sounds good to you three?" Brayden said, looking at the kids and me, ignoring her obvious friskiness. We all agreed, so Vicki wrote down our team name and told us we were all set. As Brayden turned around to leave, I noticed she was still checking him out from behind—tilting her head to get a better view.

We were the last ones to register, and we went to join all the other teams standing in front of the crowd. The four of us waved at Sam, standing off to the side with the other volunteers.

A shorter man with a stocky build and receding hairline stepped forward and cleared his throat. "Welcome everyone to this year's snowman competition!" His accent was clearly Bostonian.

The crowd cheered and clapped with contagious enthusiasm.

"We have eleven teams this year—a new record."

The crowd responded even louder, and all the people grouped in teams waved at the audience and high-fived each other.

"Every team has been provided a scarf, a hat, and a carrot. Everything else is up to your creativity. You will have thirty minutes to build your snowman, and then we will start the judging." He raised his hand in the air. "On your marks...Get set...Go!" He swung his arm down, and all the teams ran to claim their spot.

Brayden grabbed my hand and said, "Let's go this way." He pulled me to the station at the end, the kids running behind us. Kyle and Cassidy excitedly picked up our box when we got there and tipped it over, eager to check out the contents. We had a long, crooked carrot and a dark green top hat—and I gasped with excitement when I saw our scarf. It was pink and gray plaid.

I picked it up, flipped it playfully around my neck, and said to Brayden, "You picked the perfect station for us. This scarf is just my style." He smiled at me—still clearly entertained by my quirkiness.

Then he took charge, looking at the kids. "Okay, you two. We're going to start by making three snowballs. Each of you make one, and Sunny and I will do the third one together."

He crouched down beside me—his face so close to mine that I could feel his warm breath on my cheek. I watched as he silently wrapped his hands around mine, the black of his gloves contrasting with the pink of my mittens, and he guided me as we gathered up some snow together. His hands lingered on mine for a few extra seconds until the kids were in front of us, proudly showing off what they had made.

"Those look great, kids," I praised.

"Now you want to pack your snowballs nice and tight—like this." They did as they were shown, then he said, "Okay, start rolling your snowballs until they get nice and big. Sunny and I will be working on ours. Let us know if you need any help."

We started rolling our snowball, our hands working in unison, when he noticed me smiling at him. "What?" he asked me.

"It's really sweet the way you give them direction and encouragement and then let them do it on their own, instead of jumping in and doing it for them," I said, admiring how he talked to his niece and nephew.

"I think it's important for kids to do things for themselves." He thought about it for a second before continuing, "But I guess I'm like that with everyone. I give them a little guidance and let their imaginations do the rest. It's funny what people can come up with on their own when given a chance." He smiled at me, his blue eyes sparkling. "Besides, I really like the partner I'm working with."

We now had three giant snowballs, and Brayden said to the kids, "Now you need to go and gather sticks for his arms and rocks for his eyes and mouth. Sunny and I will stay here and start putting him together."

The kids ran off, excited about their new task, as Brayden turned to me and said, "Ours is the largest, so it will be the base." We rolled our snowball together for a few feet, positioning it on a flat spot at our station. "Kyle's is next." He walked over to what looked like a rather impressive snowball—considering a young child had made it. I watched as he lowered down and put his arms around it, then he stood up quickly—as if it weighed nothing at all.

He walked back toward me, and I helped him straighten it out on top of ours. My eyes stayed on him as he went over to get Cassidy's. I kept admiring the view from behind each time he walked away—noticing that he looked just as desirable from the back as he did from the front. I really couldn't blame Vicki for checking him out so much—but I chuckled a little to myself, thinking about how obviously she went about it. He smiled at me as he walked back in my direction, and I found myself even more attracted to him—impressed by his strength. He put the head on our snowman as the kids came running back, excited to show us what they had found. After setting down the sticks they were each carrying, they emptied their coat pockets.

"Wow, you guys," I said as I surveyed the items. "You found a lot of treasures."

"Yeah, we found a bunch of cool rocks," Kyle said.

"This one looks like a heart." Cassidy proudly held out her hand. "It's my favorite one." She carefully placed it on the ground.

"What's the tennis ball for?" Brayden picked up what seemed like a rather unusual item for a snowman.

"Some older kids were playing catch with it while we were looking for rocks," Kyle explained. "They dropped it when they were leaving, and Cassidy ran over and picked it up and brought it back to them, but they told her to keep it."

"That's okay, right, Uncle Brayden?"

He smiled at his niece. "Yes, Cassidy, it's okay."

"Then we found this stick with little twigs on the end that look like fingers." Kyle picked up one of the sticks and handed it to Brayden. "We want to put the tennis ball in his hand so he looks like he's playing catch."

Brayden set the tennis ball on top of the twigs. "I see what you mean." Then he looked at me and said, "This is why I let them use their imaginations." He set everything back down on the ground, turned to the kids, and said, "This sounds like a great plan, guys. Where do we want to start?"

"His face!" Cassidy exclaimed.

Brayden picked her up so she was level with the top snowball, and I handed the rocks to her. She gave him eyes and a big smile, and then I handed her the carrot. Once his face was done, Brayden asked Kyle, "Do you want to put on his hat?"

"Yeah!" He excitedly grabbed it. "Green is my favorite color." Brayden lifted him, and he put the hat on—making sure it was nice and straight.

After setting Kyle down, Brayden looked at me—grinning as he realized our scarf was still wrapped around my neck. "I think Sunny should put his scarf on. What do you guys think?" The kids agreed, so I took our scarf off and carefully tied it around our snowman's neck. Then a thought occurred to me.

"Cassidy, where's your rock that looks like a heart?"

"Right here." She picked it up from where she had set it earlier.

"Would you like to put it on his chest?" I asked, rear-ranging the scarf.

"That sounds like a great idea," Brayden said, as he helped to steady her while she stood on her tiptoes to reach where she wanted it. "Now for his arms."

Kyle picked up the stick that was going to hold the tennis ball and went to one side when his sister stopped him. "No, that one needs to go on his other side so he can be left-handed, like me and Uncle Brayden."

"We're the only two lefties in the family," he said to me, giving his niece a high-five.

I looked at Kyle. "Well, then I think we should let your sister and your uncle put his left arm on together, and you can do his right arm. How does that sound?" I held the other stick out to him, and he willingly traded with me.

Brayden put his arm around my shoulders, leaned in, and whispered, "Thank you." We shared a smile, then the three of us watched as Kyle put his stick in our snowman's right side. I handed Brayden the other stick, and Cassidy picked up the tennis ball. They stepped forward, and he gave our snowman his left arm, ensuring his hand was facing up. Brayden lifted Cassidy, who very gently placed the ball in his hand, and they came back over to Kyle and me.

With a minute to spare, we stood back and admired our work. It indeed was a team effort. It was the most creative snowman I had ever seen and a reflection of the four of us. We gave the kids high-fives, and Brayden bent down and wrapped his arms around me, pulling me in for a tight hug. Being this close to him, I caught his scent—aftershave mixed with something fresh and outdoorsy. When he let me go, our faces were just a few inches from each other—and my eyes were once again locked on his. After a long moment, I watched as his focus slowly moved down to my lips—making my eyes do the same—and a frenzy of butterflies came to life in my stomach as I imagined what it would be like to kiss him. I was pulled from my fantasy when I heard a voice next to us.

"Grandpa—his head!"

Patrick, Danielle, and their grandkids had built their snowman next to ours. I looked over at them just as their top snowball came tumbling down to the ground, leaving them with only two-thirds of a snowman. Brayden ran over and picked it up off the ground, putting it back in place for them. He quickly helped them with their hat, scarf, and face, just as we heard a voice say, "Three...Two...One."

The five of them stepped back—all with their hands in the air—and waited. It looked like everything was going to stay in place this time.

"Thanks, Brayden!" They all seemed to say it together.

"You're welcome," he told them as he found himself caught in a group hug.

After they let him go, he came back to stand beside me. "That was so sweet of you to help them." I admired his willingness to help the competition.

"That's what friends are for," he replied with a smile.

A SUNNY DAY IN WINTER

I turned from Brayden to a cheering crowd. The competition was over, and now it was time for judging. A group of three people walked around with pens and clipboards, making notes about each snowman. When they were done, they went up front and handed a piece of paper to the announcer.

"Ladies and gentlemen, we have our top three teams."

Everyone cheered and clapped again.

"In third place, we have 'The Book Club Ladies.'"

A group of four middle-aged females smiled and waved at the applause.

"In second place, we have 'The American Legion.'"

Four men wearing hats representing various military branches saluted the audience, whose cheers were even louder now.

"And in first place, we have 'Something Sweet Bakery!'"

The kids started screaming excitedly as Brayden and I smiled and waved at the crowd. Then I bent down to hug Cassidy while Brayden fist bumped Kyle. The announcer called us up front and presented us with a trophy, which the kids immediately claimed. Many people from the audience and fellow competitors came up to congratulate us, and Patrick expressed his gratitude to Brayden one last time.

"Let's go take a picture with our snowman," Brayden suggested as the crowd dispersed.

Sam walked with the four of us over to our winning entry, and Brayden said to Kyle, "Why don't you put the trophy down on the ground in front of him." Then he handed his phone to Sam, took Cassidy by the hand, and led her to the stick holding the tennis ball. "Cassidy and I will stand on this side if you and Kyle want to be on his other side," he said to me. I also handed my phone to Sam, then I took Kyle's hand and went to our suggested spot. With the kids standing so they were looking out over his arms, Brayden and I stood next to each other, our snowman in the middle.

"Say cheese," Sam told us.

"Cheese!" All four of us said together.

First, Sam took pictures with Brayden's phone, and then he held mine up as we all stayed smiling. He started to lower my phone like he was done, but then he raised his hands back up quickly—slightly changing the angle of the view. Brayden and I were pulled around to the front by the kids as they excitedly ran to grab our trophy. When I looked up at Sam, I noticed he was smiling at the image in his hand, and Brayden and I thanked him as we took back our phones. I put mine in my coat pocket, figuring I would have plenty of time later to check out the pictures. Right now, I would rather focus on the man in front of me than on my phone. Kyle and Cassidy scampered off, heading back to the bakery's tent to share our good news with April and Lauren, with Sam following them.

"Thanks for helping the kids and me," Brayden said to me as we admired our snowman one more time.

"I had a lot of fun. And it's not every day I get to build a snowman with a now four-time champion," I replied with a playful tone. I glanced over at him and noticed he was still looking at our snowman, his eyes full of nostalgia.

He gave a little laugh. "Yeah, this does bring back some good memories of when April and I were kids." After a moment, he turned to look at me with a soft smile. "Would you like to have lunch with me at the bakery, Sunny?"

"Thanks, Brayden, that sounds nice." My smile mirrored his, happy for the invitation to spend more time with him.

Chapter 5

♥

THE BAKERY WAS WARM and inviting after being out in the cold. It smelled just as good as earlier. We were greeted by a pretty blonde behind the counter. She wore the same pink and white striped apron Lauren and April had on this morning, complemented by a purple sweater underneath. She smiled when she saw us come in.

"Hi, Brayden. Congratulations on winning the snowman competition. That tennis ball idea sounded so creative."

"Thanks, it really was." Then he gestured to me and said, "This is Sunny. She helped the kids and me. We couldn't have won without her."

I beamed at his compliment. "The four of us made a great team!"

"This is Marissa," Brayden said to me. "She's been with us since we first opened the bakery."

"It's nice to meet you," I said to her.

"You too. Are you guys here for lunch?"

A SUNNY DAY IN WINTER

I noticed that a new chalkboard was now on display, listing the lunch offerings.

"We branched out into making sandwiches a while ago. This way, we have something to offer the lunch crowd. People can also try my sister's bread and then buy it to take home with them."

"Brayden here is always thinking up new ways to grow the business," Marissa said to me. "He always has his nose stuck in his computer."

My focus switched to the chalkboard, with the same pretty handwriting and colorful chalk as the other signs. There was a name next to each sandwich:

The Lauren: Tuna Melt on Whole Wheat
The April: Turkey, Avocado, and Bacon on White
The Sam: Classic Rueben on Rye
The Kyle: Turkey and Cheddar on White
The Marissa: Egg Salad and Tomato on Sourdough
The Alex: BLT on Whole Wheat

Who's Alex? I wondered as my eyes moved down to the following line that read:

Kid's Menu:
The Cassidy: Grilled Cheese on White
The Brayden: Peanut Butter and Raspberry Jam on Sourdough

Marissa must have noticed the amused look on my face as I read that last item because she said, "Yes, our resident bachelor still hasn't progressed past peanut butter and jelly."

I looked at Brayden, and he just shrugged. "It's a classic."

"Would you like your usual?" Marissa asked him.

"Not today, thanks. I didn't have time for breakfast this morning. My mom made those coffee cups sound so urgent." He shook his head and looked at me. "And what was her deal with telling me to shave and dress nicely only to send me out to build a snowman? I don't get it." He ran his hand through his hair like he was trying to figure it out as he said, "I'll have a coffee and a cinnamon roll. Thanks, Marissa."

"How about you, Sunny?"

I looked at the menu board again. "I will have 'The Cassidy' and a cup of coffee, please."

We both looked at the pastry cabinet and noticed the space for chocolate cake with chocolate frosting was still empty. Seeing the disappointment on his face, Marissa said, "Sorry, Brayden, I know it's your favorite."

"It's Sunny's favorite, too," he said, smiling at me.

"But don't worry, we have a new one in the oven. When your sister realized she had forgotten the baking soda, we had to toss the first one out."

"I can relate to that," I empathized. "When I was in the sixth grade, I made bread in home ec class with confectioner's sugar instead of flour. My bread was stuck in the pan so bad that I had to scrape it out with a knife. And it looked nothing like bread."

They both looked at me wide-eyed.

"How on earth did that happen?" Brayden asked as they were both laughing.

"The flour and confectioner's sugar were on the table next to each other in unmarked containers," I said, sounding like a squeaky chicken again. "They looked exactly the same!"

The bright smile that kept appearing on his face once again returned.

"What?" I squeaked.

"You're cute when you're flustered," he said, his eyes alight with enjoyment as he watched me.

"You two go have a seat." Marissa slid our coffees across the counter, giving Brayden a curious look. "I'll bring your food over when it's ready."

Brayden put his free hand on the small of my back and led me to a table I hadn't noticed before. It was tucked in a corner out of the way of everything else—cozy and intimate. The gas fireplace in the wall made it feel even more romantic, and I smiled when I saw the flowers were different. Where all the other tables had pink and white carnations, this one had five pink tulips in a small vase—making it feel even more special.

We set our coffees down, took off our coats and scarves, and Brayden pulled my chair out for me. There was a single hook on the wall behind his chair, and I watched as he grabbed our scarves. He intertwined them and hung them up. Then, he draped our coats over the top of them—his covering mine. I loved how our coats and scarves looked hanging up on the wall together—like they belonged that way.

Without his coat on, I could see the rest of his out-fit—a navy-blue sweater with the collar and cuffs of a button-down shirt peeking out at his neck and wrists. I now understood his point in not being dressed to build a snowman. I didn't bother to tell him who had typed the message. I just smiled as I took in his handsome appear-ance.

"This is my favorite spot in the entire bakery. It's so private over here," he said as he sat down across from me.

"I know—it's like we have the whole place to ourselves," I agreed with a smile, my eyes landing on his. "And this fireplace makes it so warm and cozy." The bakery felt dif-ferent to me now than it did this morning. And it wasn't just the fireplace that made it feel so warm and cozy. It was really because of the man sitting across from me.

A few minutes later, Marissa appeared next to us. "Here you go." She set down our plates and looked at Brayden for a long moment.

"What?" he asked her.

"There is something so different about you today," she said with a thoughtful pause—her blue eyes studying his face. "I've never seen you like this before. It's about time you look happy." She turned and smiled at me. "You are having quite the effect on our serious bossman here, Sunny." She gave my shoulder a grateful squeeze. Then she headed back to the counter.

I felt a wave of happiness flood through me. Based on how Marissa acted, it was like I was bringing some sunshine into Brayden's life. And that's precisely what I do best.

WE WERE ENJOYING THE first few bites of our food when April came rushing over and shoved Brayden's plate out of the way, setting a laptop down right in front of him.

"Hey, I was eating that!" he said, looking at his sister with a very annoyed expression.

"Yeah, yeah, yeah, I need your help Brady," she said urgently. She looked across the table at me, and her face relaxed to a smile, her tone much more cheerful as she spoke to me. "Hi, Sunny."

"Pulling out the 'Brady,' are we?" He raised his eyebrows at his sister. Then he looked at me and said, "My sister only ever calls me 'Brady' if she's messed something up and wants to get back on my good side."

"I was trying to update the spreadsheet you set up earlier when the screen went blank." There was a nervous tone to her voice.

"This is why I tell you and Mom to leave the financial stuff up to me," he said, studying his computer. "I don't go into the kitchen and do your job, do I?"

"Thankfully, no," April said, looking at me. "Brayden once made cinnamon rolls with too much salt when we were kids."

"Oh, really?" I asked, with the same amused tone he gave me earlier. "How on earth did that happen?"

"What? Tablespoon; teaspoon...what's the difference?" He glanced up at me with a playful look in his eyes.

"So, tell me, April," I said, looking back at her. "How were these cinnamon rolls of his?"

"Oh, they were so horrible we had to throw them out. Mom banished him from the kitchen after that."

Brayden gave his sister that annoyed look of his again. "Don't you have work to do in the kitchen?" I found their sibling banter amusing, but I don't think he appreciated his sister spilling his culinary secrets.

She looked down at his computer. "So, do you think you can fix it?"

"I'm not sure," Brayden answered, his eyes back on the screen. "What were you doing touching my computer anyway?"

"You're the one who left it here. I was just trying to help," she said defensively with her hands in the air.

"I guess I should update my password then," he muttered.

As he was busy typing, April turned her attention back to me. "Kyle and Cassidy were so excited to win the snowman competition."

"We had so much fun. Thanks again for asking me to join them." Then I glanced at Brayden and said with a playful tone, "And I met your brother's girlfriend."

His fingers stopped typing, and he looked up at me—his eyebrows furrowed in confusion. "My girlfriend?"

I looked at April and said, "A burgundy-haired lady of a certain age couldn't keep her heavily made-up green eyes off your brother."

"Vicki and her x-ray vision," she teased her brother as she playfully batted at him with her apron strings. Then she turned to me and said, "Or so she wishes."

Brayden ran both hands through his hair and shook his head. "That woman is something else."

"Vicki is well known around town as being a cougar, and she's been trying to get her paws on Brayden ever since she first met him," April said to me, laughing. "I used to work with her. My brother stopped by the office one day, and she spent the whole time checking him out and flirting with him. As soon as he left, Vicki asked me if he was single, so I asked her if she thought Brayden might be a little young for her. She just waved her hand and said, 'Honey, your brother is the perfect age. He's old enough to be legal but still young enough that I could have fun teaching him a few things.'"

Brayden's jaw dropped as he stared at his sister—his eyes wide with horror. "She said that to you?"

"Yup, she did. And whenever he would stop by, Vicki would always hang out at my desk and flirt with him."

"That's because a certain somebody always made it a point to tell her I was there." He crossed his arms and raised his eyebrows at his sister.

"I don't know who you're talking about," she said, putting her hand over her heart and feigning innocence.

He just shook his head and went back to concentrating on his computer.

"So, did I mess it up really bad?" April asked him, nervously fidgeting with her rings.

"You did," he answered matter-of-factly. He glanced at his anxious business partner, and his entire demeanor changed as soon as he noticed her hands. The tension melted from his face; he leaned back in his chair, looked at her very calmly, and said, "But it's just a spreadsheet, right?"

"Yeah, it's just a spreadsheet," she echoed, relieved but also confused. She stood there and stared at her brother for a moment like she was having difficulty making sense of his reaction. Then, she shot me a look I didn't quite understand before she turned and headed back toward the kitchen.

Brayden had gone back to his typing, and after a minute, he looked at me over the top of his computer. "What?" he asked, seeing the amused grin on my face.

"Nice laptop cover."

"Oh, that," he sighed. It had a light blue background with donuts all over it, covered in pink and white frosting and brightly colored sprinkles. "This was a total compromise with my sister. She made me put this on my computer since I refuse to wear one of those foo-foo aprons she insisted on getting."

"I think it's sweet that you let your sister do that to your poor computer," I teased.

"I've been trying for years to get her to leave my stuff alone, but I guess that's never going to happen." He closed his laptop and set it aside, moving his plate back to where it belonged. "Fixing her mistake can wait until later. Right now, I want to get back to why we're really here—having lunch with you."

Chapter 6

♥

A LITTLE WHILE LATER, our lunch finished, we were still sitting quietly in our cozy little nook of the bakery. The fireplace continued to set a very romantic mood as we enjoyed learning more about each other.

"So, what made your family decide to open a bakery?"

"My sister always enjoyed cooking and baking growing up—she was never banished from the kitchen like I was," Brayden laughed. "She always dreamed of opening a bakery. She even went to culinary school."

"What did you do before starting the bakery?" I asked him.

"After studying economics at Syracuse, I went to New York City and worked in the financial district for a few years. Then I came back to Vermont a little while ago." After a pause, he said, "What about you, Sunny? What sorts of adventures did life take you on?"

"I joined the military after high school. I did my four years of Active Duty in the Air Force, and then I eventually made my way back home as well. I went to massage therapy school a few years ago and work in a local spa now."

"You were in the Air Force?" He had a surprised look on his face. "I would not have pictured you in the military."

"Yeah, I get that a lot," I said with a little laugh. "Between the makeup and the bright and cheerful outfits, nothing about me screams 'Veteran.'"

"Well, you're definitely the cutest Veteran I've ever seen," he said, smiling at me. "What did you do in the service?"

"I worked in communications. Answering phones, talking on the radios." I shook my head good-naturedly. "Those poor aircrews, having to listen to me squeak at them over the airwaves. One of the mission commanders even admitted to me that they would all laugh whenever they heard my voice." Even when I don't sound like a squeaky chicken, my voice is still relatively high-pitched.

"I'm sure it was all in good fun. You have a very friendly tone to your voice."

"Thanks, Brayden." I smiled at his compliment. I've enjoyed listening to his voice all day—his pitch being the exact opposite of mine. I love hearing a deep voice on a man, and his was sexy enough to rival that of Morgan Freeman himself. "And thanks for not asking me if I flew planes," I added with a laugh. "Whenever someone asks me that, I always respond with, 'No, but I did outrank Chuck Norris!'"

He laughed and tilted his head to the side as he looked at me for a long moment, his face relaxing to a content smile. "You are one of a kind, Sunny Jackson. I'm really enjoying getting to know you."

"Me too, Brayden." Warmth radiated through me as I got lost in his soft, glowing eyes—grateful to have met a man who appreciates my unique personality.

Our quiet moment was interrupted by two energetic kids running up to our table.

"Uncle Brayden, Mom's going to take us sliding at Mr. Beauchamp's farm!" Kyle said excitedly.

"You and Sunny have to come with us." Cassidy climbed onto Brayden's lap as he pushed his chair back to give her more room.

"We do?" he asked them in an animated tone.

"Uh-huh," she answered as she grabbed our gloves and mittens from the table's edge.

Kyle was trying to get our coats and scarves down off the hook, but he wasn't quite tall enough to reach. His solution was to get under Brayden's coat and keep jumping up to try and unhook it, and when it finally did break free, it landed on top of his sister and uncle. He did the same thing with my coat, and after a few tries, it landed on our table, taking up the entire surface. Then he pulled down our scarves, came around the table, and flipped them over my head. As soon as Brayden's scarf landed on me, I picked up his scent again. I discreetly slid one side around the front of my neck and over my shoulder—instantly making all of my senses come to life as if he was right in front of me again.

"I guess we're going sliding," I said to Brayden, laughing at Cassidy's hair flying all around from the static, as he had just uncovered them and set his coat on top of mine.

"I guess so." He smiled as he noticed I was wearing our intertwined scarves.

Just then, April showed up, and Kyle said, "Mom, Uncle Brayden, and Sunny are coming with us."

She laughed when she saw our coats piled up on the table and our scarves draped around my neck. "I see you've been helping them get ready."

"Mommy, can we ride with Uncle Brayden and Sunny?" Cassidy asked.

"I'm not the one you need to ask." April looked at her brother.

All Cassidy had to do was look at Brayden, and we all knew the answer. "Of course, you guys can ride with us," he said, kissing her on top of her head. She got off his lap and excitedly tugged at his arm to get him out of his seat. The two of us stood, and he took our coats off the table—only to discover that the little vase with the tulips had unfortunately been tipped over.

"I'll give these some new water, and hopefully, they'll be okay," April said, grabbing the vase. "We'll be ready to go in a few minutes. Sam's just bringing the tent in from outside."

As she turned back toward the kitchen, Brayden asked her to hold on as he picked up his laptop and handed it to her. "Can you take this and put it in the kitchen, please?" As she was leaving, he called after her, "And no opening it this time." She just smiled innocently over her shoulder at him as she walked away.

Brayden was about to put his coat on when he stopped and looked at me—his eyes sparkling as he focused on our scarves still around my neck. He watched as I gradually untwisted them—in no rush to give his back. Every time I breathed in, I secretly indulged in his scent, purposely brushing the warm thickness across my face with each pass. He slowly pulled his scarf off my outstretched hand and remained looking at me as he put it on—his eyes not leaving mine.

I was pulled back to reality as Cassidy excitedly put my coat in my hand and said, "Here, Sunny." I thanked her as I smiled at the two young faces, happy to have a new friend.

As we headed to the kitchen, we walked by Marissa, who smiled at us and said, "Have fun." She grabbed Brayden's shoulders and gave him a little shake. "Especially you."

Cassidy led the way as we stepped out the back door, taking her uncle's hand and excitedly pulling him along. After a few steps, I felt a hand in mine, and I looked down to see Kyle's green mitten tucked inside my pink one. April, Sam, and Lauren smiled and waved as they slowly drove past us—their eyes widening with disbelief as they all noticed my new little friend.

"April and I used to go sliding at Mr. Beauchamp's all the time when we were kids." Brayden's voice pulled my attention to him. "He has a rather large farm just off the turnpike."

Now it was my turn to be surprised. "Vermont has a turnpike?"

"Yup, we do," he replied with a grin. "I'm guessing you've never been on it?"

"No, I didn't realize our little rural state even had one." I associate turnpikes with large interstates in significant cities, and Vermont's big city of Burlington has about thirty thousand residents—so not exactly huge. I will admit that he has certainly captured my interest and curiosity.

When we got to a black Volvo, the kids opened the back doors, popped up the built-in booster seats, and climbed in—Kyle behind Brayden and Cassidy behind me. Three of us silently listened as a chatty little girl entertained us with her stories. I glanced back at Kyle a few times and noticed how he seemed content to let his sister do all the talking as he just looked out his window. Brayden and I shared a smile, and he quietly said to me, "This is typical for these two."

After we crossed a set of railroad tracks, Brayden turned right off Route 11. I looked at him wide-eyed and said, "*This* is the Green Mountain Turnpike?"

"It is indeed," he replied with a huge grin.

"But it's a dirt road!"

"We have our little quirks here in Chester—just like you have in Westminister."

"Good point," I said, smiling at him.

Cassidy was still jabbering away in the backseat as we made our way down the country turnpike and took a sharp turn leading up a very steep driveway. As we were making our way up the hill, Brayden said, "There's a huge bank leading down to the pasture, and Mr. Beauchamp always corrals his Scottish Highlanders during the Winter Carnival so families can have fun here without running into his cows."

"I'm sure his cows appreciate that," I said with a little laugh.

"I get to ride with Uncle Brayden first," Kyle said, practically pulling him out of his seat as soon as we were parked.

I opened my door to see Cassidy standing beside me—her face alight as she grabbed my hand. "Come on, Sunny!"

We joined April, Sam, and Lauren at the top of the hill, chatting with the other parents while they waited for us. The fresh, deep snow was perfect for an afternoon of winter fun, and the four of us piled into two sleds—Kyle in between Brayden's knees and Cassidy between mine.

"Do you want to race?" Brayden challenged me with a competitive grin.

"Last one down is a rotten egg!" I pushed us off and wrapped my arms around Cassidy. We got down to the bottom and looked back to see the guys were two-thirds down the hill.

"We won!" Cassidy exclaimed, jumping out of the sled.

"That's because we weigh more than you two," Brayden said as they came to a stop next to us.

"A win is a win," I said as I gave Cassidy a congratulatory high-five.

"Let's go again!" Kyle yelled as he and his sister ran back up the hill.

After grabbing the ropes for both sleds, Brayden took my hand, and we walked back up the hill together, laughing whenever one of us would lose our footing in the snow and slip a little bit. April and Lauren were smiling as they watched us, clearly happy to see everyone having such a great time.

We spent a little while taking turns sliding with the kids, April and Sam joining in as well. Lauren designated herself the official photographer, capturing the fun her grandkids were having.

Brayden and I had ridden a few times down the hill together, sometimes him in front, sometimes me. We were now at a steeper part of the bank, and no one else was around. As much as I enjoyed being with his family, I welcomed the privacy as I climbed into the sled and sat down between his legs. I leaned back against his chest as he wrapped his strong arms around me, his breath warming the side of my face.

"Are you ready for this, Jackson?" he asked as we teetered on the slope's edge.

I took a deep breath. "Ready."

He pushed us off with his hands and then clamped his arms right back around me. We picked up speed as we flew down our snowy rollercoaster, both screaming like kids. It was scary and exhilarating, and I gripped Brayden's arms, squeezing them tighter against me. The sled turned when we were almost at the bottom, and we both went tumbling out, rolling the last few yards until we came to a stop next to each other where the ground leveled out. He rolled onto his side and propped himself up on his elbow, trying to contain his growing laughter when he saw how much snow was covering me.

"Are you okay?"

"Yeah," I answered through my giggling. "I'm great. That was so much fun!"

He removed his glove and gently brushed the snow from my face—his warm touch comforting my cold skin. He held my gaze for a moment, our childlike laughter calming to quiet smiles. His handsome face shielded my eyes from the mid-afternoon sun, and the halo of rays encircling his snowy hair brought to mind a fond memory.

"You know what I haven't done in a long time? Made a snow angel. I made those all the time when I was a kid."

"Let's do it!" he said as he rolled a couple of feet from me. Our hands and feet kept making contact as we moved them in and out, pushing the snow aside. After several passes, I sprang to my feet, grabbing his hand on my way and pulling him to stand next to me.

"They look like they're holding hands," I chirped, wrapping my hands around his as I admired our wintry couple.

"You're just as cute when you're excited as you are when you're flustered," Brayden complimented me, his voice alive with entertainment. I glanced at him to discover that he wasn't looking at our snow angels. Instead, he watched me with that amused smile that brightened up his face every time my unique personality traits came out. A big clump of snow falling off the back of my coat redirected his attention, and he gave a little laugh as he looked down at our frosty sweethearts.

As he brushed the snow off my back, he said, "So, I've been meaning to ask you. 'Sunny'...Is that a nickname?"

"It is." My smile grew bigger as I thought about the origins of my nickname. "I was born in the winter, and it had been snowing and sleeting as my dad took my mom to the hospital that morning. The sky was all dark and overcast, but as soon as I was born, the clouds instantly cleared up, and the sun came out. Even the doctor and nurses commented on how the room suddenly brightened right up at my arrival into the world. The nurse put me on my mom and said, 'Meet your new little ray of sunshine.' And even though my parents already knew for months what they would name me, they began calling me 'Sunny.' That's how I've been known for my entire life, and nice weather still follows me to this day." After a second, I added with a laugh, "The only one who wasn't excited about the new ray of sunshine was my brother, but he eventually got over it, and now we get along just fine."

Brayden was listening to my story with a smile that mirrored mine, but after a minute, his expression changed. It was like he was piecing together various clues throughout today and just now realizing something.

"Sunny?" he asked quietly, reaching out and taking my hands. "Is today your birthday?"

"Maybe," I said shyly.

"Why didn't you tell us?"

"You and your family have been so sweet and welcoming to me all day. What more could you possibly do?"

He kept hold of one of my hands and started leading me back up the hill, pulling our sled behind.

"So, what's your real name?"

"Sydney. But people only call me that if I'm in trouble. And if I hear 'Sydney Michaela,' then I know I'm really in trouble!"

Chapter 7

As soon as we returned to the top of the hill and re-joined Brayden's family, Cassidy ran up and grabbed my hand, pulling me over to her sled.

"You and me against Kyle and Daddy!"

"Let's show these two how it's done," I exclaimed as Cassidy took her seat in front of me.

Sam counted us down, and we both pushed off as Lauren took out her phone to get a picture of our race.

We got down to the bottom of the hill and looked back up. Sam and Kyle were only halfway down, so we were even faster this time.

"Still the champions," I said to the guys as they slid up next to us.

"No fair," Kyle protested. "Dad's even heavier than Uncle Brayden."

"Sorry, kiddo," I said with an encouraging smile.

The four of us got out of the sleds, and as we were making our way back up the hill, I asked Kyle if he wanted to ride down with me next—figuring the poor kid could use a win. So, we agreed to switch partners, and before we sat down, I asked Lauren to make sure to get a picture of us as we got to the bottom of the hill. Sam counted us down again, and as soon as we pushed ourselves off, I wrapped my arms around my hopeful rider. When we got to the bottom, I looked back and noticed that our competition was about three-quarters of the way down, and I breathed out a sigh of relief that Kyle had gotten his win. When they arrived next to us, Sam congratulated his son and gave him a high-five. The kids jumped out of the sleds, and Kyle had a huge smile on his face—so proud of his victory. The kids ran back up the hill, with Sam and me a few steps behind them.

"Thanks for suggesting we switch partners. Kyle really wanted to win, and there was no way that was going to happen with Brayden or me," he said with a laugh as we pulled our sleds behind us. "Kyle's not as outgoing as his sister, and I think a lot of the time he's okay being the one in the background, but April and I like it when he gets to be in the spotlight."

"I figured out pretty quickly after meeting your kids just how different they are. On the ride here, Kyle sat and looked out his window while Cassidy chatted the whole time—the rest of us couldn't get a word in edgewise."

Sam laughed again and said, "Yeah, sometimes I think Kyle's the smartest one out of all of us. His natural tendency to stay quiet keeps him out of trouble—especially when April gets on a tear about something. I don't know if the rest of us will ever learn."

When we arrived at the top of the hill, Lauren showed us the pictures she had taken. Some of them were during the race—Kyle and I leading the way down the mountain—and then a few showed us at the bottom first. My shy new friend was still beaming at having won a friendly competition with his sister—who seemed unfazed by coming in second.

After a little more pleading from Cassidy, Lauren agreed to be the next rider with her. Giving both sleds a friendly nudge, April and I watched as her mom held onto Cassidy for dear life. I'm unsure whom she felt more afraid for—herself or her granddaughter.

"Thank you, Sunny," April said, hugging me once it was just the two of us. "It was so sweet of you to do that for Kyle."

"You're welcome, April," I said, tightening my arms around her.

When she let me go, she held my hands and said, "It is amazing to see how Kyle has really come out of his shell today. He's usually so shy around new people. I know some of it is his excitement for the carnival, but he's really taken to you. We were all surprised to see him holding your hand earlier, and then the way he agreed so quickly to ride down the hill with you—it's like he's a completely different kid." She smiled at me gratefully. "Thank you, Sunny, for making him feel so comfortable."

A warmth spread through my heart, feeling so special that such a shy little boy would warm up to me so fast—making someone else come to mind. "I see a lot of my brother in Kyle. I think that's why it's so easy for me to relate to him." I squeezed her hands as I added, "Thanks again for inviting me to spend the day with your family. I am having so much fun with everyone."

We both looked over to see everyone heading down the slope again. This time Kyle was wrapped in Lauren's tight grip while Cassidy was laughing with her dad.

When I turned back to April, there was a sparkle in her eyes as she said, "But the person I'm the happiest for today is Brayden. It's nice to see him actually having fun for once. He's always working so hard at the bakery, and Mom and I are constantly telling him he deserves a day off, but he refuses to take one. That's why we had to get him outside this morning. We knew he would have fun building the snowman with the kids."

"Cassidy seems to really love him."

A warm smile spread across her face. "They've always had a special bond, ever since she was a baby."

"She did a good job under the tent this morning convincing him to go to the snowman competition, and then he instantly agreed to her request of riding here with us."

"Yeah, it takes very little effort from her, and Brayden is hooked. We use it to our advantage a lot," she said, laughing. "My brother's not a very emotional man, and he is quite serious most of the time, but there's always been something about Cassidy that brings out the softer side in him." She was quiet for a second, then added, "And just so you know, Cassidy isn't the only one to bring out a different side of my brother. He's been a lot happier and easy-going since he met you, Sunny. We've all noticed a change in him today."

Everyone had piled into their sleds again, ready for another run down the hill, when a message beeped in on April's phone. Her face was beaming as she read it, then her expression changed to authoritative as she called out to her family, "Come on, guys. We have to go."

"Please, Mom, just one more time," Kyle pleaded.

"Sorry guys, we have to leave now. Grab your sleds, and let's head to the car."

"Will we all fit? Where did your brother go?" Lauren asked, looking around.

I had been having so much fun sliding with the kids and talking with April that I just now realized Brayden was gone.

As we walked to April's car, Cassidy said, "Mommy, where's Uncle Brayden?"

"He left for a minute."

"Why?"

"Because he did."

"Why didn't he take me with him?"

"Because he didn't," she answered as she opened the hatchback of her car for the sleds. "You and your brother—get in."

As she climbed into the third row with her brother, Cassidy was still asking questions. Lauren and I sat in the second row, and after shutting the sleds in the back, April and Sam got in the front. "See, we all fit," she said triumphantly, looking at Lauren in her rearview mirror.

"Where is your brother, honey? And why did we have to leave so quickly?" Lauren asked April as we were getting on the turnpike.

"He needed to take care of something," April said impatiently, clearly getting annoyed with all of her family's questions. Lauren just looked at me and shrugged.

It was now late afternoon, and the sun was getting lower in the sky. As we got to the center of town, April turned off Main Street, prompting Sam to ask, "Why are we going this way?"

"I need to stop by the bakery really quick," she answered.

"Why?" Lauren questioned her daughter. "Marissa should have locked up half an hour ago."

"I need to run in for something. And Sunny needs to come with me." April glanced at me in her rearview mirror.

"Why does Sunny need to go with you?" Sam asked his wife.

"Because she does." Her tone was getting more irritable with every question she answered.

"Hey—isn't that Brayden's car?" Sam asked as we drove past a black Volvo and parked a few spaces down.

"Samuel!" April snapped at him, her bulging eyes and clenched jaw signaling he should stop asking questions. Getting the hint that his wife was annoyed with him, he

64

stopped talking and looked back at Lauren, who shrugged at him with her palms in the air. "I should have left all of you at Mr. Beauchamp's farm. The only one minding his own business is Kyle." Her face softened slightly as she looked at her son in the back seat. She shifted her focus to me, and her entire demeanor instantly changed. Her posture relaxed, and the irritation was gone from her voice as she smiled at me and said, "Come on, Sunny."

I didn't say anything as I looked at Lauren—wide-eyed with confusion—hoping for an answer. She patted my hand and said, "It's best just to listen to her and do what she says when she gets like this." She put her hand to the side of her mouth, pointed at her daughter, and whispered, "Bossy pants, remember."

April glared at her mom around her seat. "I heard that, Mother." Then her eyes shifted back to me, the exasperation vanishing from her face as she reached back and gave my hand a reassuring squeeze. "It's okay Sunny. Let's go in."

April unlocked the back door, led me through the kitchen, and gently nudged me into the main room of the bakery. Before I could say anything to her, she shut the kitchen door between us and disappeared. I stared at the door for a moment, still unsure why I was there.

I turned around, and my breath caught in my throat as the most romantic sight greeted me. The lights were all off, and my eyes were immediately drawn to the ceiling. Now that there wasn't much daylight coming through the windows, the twinkling of the fairy lights overhead made the whole place feel even more magical. My attention slowly drifted to candles happily flickering on all the tables, illuminating the fresh flowers in their vases. My focus eventually landed on the floor—a line of red rose petals leading me to my ultimate destination. My eyes followed the trail to the front of the counter and off to the right side of the room. But I couldn't move. Not yet. I just stood there for a second, taking it all in—the incredible thoughtfulness that went into all of this.

Once I could finally move, I slowly made my way through the bakery—wanting to savor the moment and where it was taking me. As soon as I realized that the trail of rose petals was leading to the private nook where Brayden and I had enjoyed lunch, I looked up and saw him standing in front of our table—his eyes sparkling as he admired my reaction.

With a few quiet steps, he closed the gap between us, his handsome face aglow in the candlelight as he wrapped his arms around me. As I stood in his warm embrace, I fought back the tears, touched by the kindness of a man I had met only a few hours ago. I felt such an instant connection to him this morning, and I hoped he felt it too. He had hugged me after the snowman competition, but this time being in his arms felt different—like we weren't just celebrating a win. Now at this moment, between his kind gesture, and the way he was holding me, I knew I was very special to him. No one had ever done anything this sweet for me, and I wrapped my arms tighter around him, hoping he knew how I felt. He buried his face deeper into my neck, stroking my hair as we stayed silent the entire time—no words needing to be spoken.

His hands slid around my shoulders as he straightened up, looking at me with a soft smile. "Happy birthday Sunny."

"Thank you, Brayden," I whispered, still fighting back the tears but ultimately losing my battle. As he gently wiped the tears from my eyes, something behind him caught my attention.

The table next to the fireplace was set up with two candles, and in between was the small vase with the pink tulips from earlier—having survived being tipped over by our coats. There were two plates on either side of the table with sandwiches, two cups of coffee, and two glasses of water.

"I know it's not much—but I'm a bachelor who's been banished from the kitchen—remember?" he said with a playful smile.

"It's perfect," I said, smiling at him.

"Do you want to have a seat?"

I nodded, and he took my hand and led me over to the table. He pulled out my chair and hung up my coat and scarf over his on the hook—happiness spreading through me as I enjoyed the simple sweetness of the moment. He sat across from me, and I picked up half of my sandwich, my eyes brightening as I realized it was peanut butter with raspberry jam.

"Your specialty," I said, my smile growing more extensive as I saw the gleam in his eyes.

"When I told my sister I wanted to do this for you, she gave me a one-time pass into the kitchen—figuring I wouldn't mess anything up too badly," he said with a small laugh.

"So that text message she got when she rounded everyone up to leave was from you?"

"Yeah, she's the only one that I told it's your birthday, and I wanted to do a little celebration for you. Since I wanted to keep it a surprise, I knew I couldn't tell my mom—figuring she would get too excited and accidentally say something. And I knew that when April heard from me, she would wrangle everyone into the car and get you back here. When my sister gets her mind set on something, the best thing to do is listen to her—and we all know it."

"Your mom and Sam told me the same thing. Everyone was asking questions except Kyle. He stayed quiet the entire time."

"That is one smart kid," he said with a laugh. "So, she turned into Miss Bossy Pants?"

"She did. Your mom even called her that," I said, my laughter matching his. "I could tell she was getting impatient with all the questions. She even called poor Sam, 'Samuel.'"

He shook his head, his laughter calming to a smile. "It sounds like she was really on a roll." There was a hint of pride and accomplishment in his eyes as he tilted his head and gazed at me across the table. "I'm really happy she got you here with the surprise still intact. Once you told me it was your birthday, I knew I had to do something special for you."

"Well, I was definitely surprised. You two make quite the team." I smiled at him affectionately and reached for his hands. "Thank you so much for doing this for me."

After our sandwiches were finished, Brayden stood up from the table, grabbed our plates, and headed toward the kitchen. While he was gone, I looked fondly at the candles and tulips on our table and throughout the rest of the bakery. Now that the sun had officially set, the fairy lights and the candles everywhere really lit the place up—making it feel even more romantic and intimate. I still couldn't believe he had done all this for me. He was making me feel truly special.

He appeared a minute later holding two plates with slices of chocolate cake with chocolate frosting—one with a candle in it—which he placed in front of me. After setting down his plate, he leaned in, kissed me on the cheek, and said, "Make a wish, Sunny."

Looking at him sitting across from me, I realized I didn't need to wish for anything. Something in his eyes was telling me that all of my dreams had come true when I met him this morning. It felt so right to be in his presence—like I was destined to meet him. And based on the way he hugged me earlier and the emotion I felt in his embrace, I got the sense that he knew it too. So, I smiled at him, closed my eyes, and blew out my candle—silently thanking the universe for the unexpected gift it had sent me this morning. I opened my eyes to see the same things mirrored on his face—like he was reading my mind.

I took my first bite of cake, and my eyelids slowly fluttered shut as I let the chocolatey goodness linger for a long moment of indulgence. The sweetness of the cake contrasted beautifully with the slightly bitter, darker chocolate of the frosting—the opposing flavors complementing each other perfectly. I let out a sigh of contentment, a smile spreading across my face as my favorite birthday treat melted in my mouth.

"Not bad, huh?" Brayden's voice pulled me from my reverie.

I opened my eyes to see him smiling at me, his eyes sparkling with happiness as he watched me.

"This is the best cake I have ever tasted," I said, my smile glowing.

"Thanks, Sunny. I'm glad you like it. My sister uses our grandmother's recipe."

"Her cake definitely lives up to the reviews."

He reached across the table and took my hands, his smile relaxing to one of contentment. "I'm even more grateful now for all those reviews since they're what brought you here this morning."

I looked down at our hands—noticing how well they fit together. "And it's not just the food that gets such great reviews either. So many people raved about the wonderful family who owns the bakery—but I had no idea just how true that was until I got here. My morning kept getting better and better with each person I met." I paused briefly, lifting my eyes back to his face. "And they saved the best family member for last."

We shared a long, silent moment in our romantic little corner of the world—where nothing else seemed to matter. As I looked at him sitting across the table from me—his blue eyes glowing with happiness—I also felt very grateful for all those beautiful reviews that brought me here. And as amazing as the cake is, it doesn't hold a candle to the sweet man I'm sharing it with.

"So, tell me about your family," he said as we returned to enjoying our favorite dessert. "You mentioned having a brother earlier. Do you have any nieces or nephews?"

"No—but he is married, and he and his wife have a cat."

He laughed and said, "That seems to be a trend in your family."

"Yeah, we joke that we have furry nieces. Kyle and Cassidy remind me a lot of my brother and me. He's always been shy and quiet, and I'm the friendly and chatty one. He takes after our mom, and I take after our dad."

"Does he live in Westminister too?"

I nodded. "He lives closer to my parents than I do, and we all see each other quite often. Not as much as you and your sister, however. I don't think Russ and I could own a business together. We are way too different and would drive each other crazy."

"April and I have opposite personalities too, but that's part of why we work so well together. We might bicker sometimes, but there's no one else I'd rather have as a business partner. So, are you working at the spa tomorrow?"

"I am. I work most weekend days—which I'm sure you can relate to."

"Yeah, but at least being the numbers guy, I don't have to be in as early as my sister, and I can do a lot of my work when the bakery is closed. I don't know how she gets up to be here at four-thirty every morning," he said, shaking his head. "I am certainly not a morning person."

"I work the early shift at the spa, but I don't start nearly as early as your sister. My first massage is at nine tomorrow, and I know I'm fully booked with appointments."

He pulled out his phone, and his eyes widened as he looked at the screen.

"Would you believe it's ten-thirty already?" he asked me.

"Really?" I've been enjoying his company so much that I lost track of time. Not that I was in any rush to leave.

"Yeah," he said with a sigh. "If you need to get heading home, I understand."

I sighed as well. "I guess I probably should. It's one thing for my clients to fall asleep during a massage, but it wouldn't be good if I did."

Brayden pulled my chair back for me, and I helped him blow out the candles and get the place ready for us to leave. He grabbed our coats and scarves and asked as we bundled up, "Where did you park this morning?"

"The large field where the volunteers directed me."

"Since it's dark, I can go with you if you'd like."

"Thanks, Brayden, that would be nice," I said, appreciating his gentlemanly offer.

We went through the kitchen, and as he locked the door, he said, "We can either walk, or I can drive us."

It was rather cold out, but it was a clear night, and the full moon cast a beautiful glow. I looked up at the sky full of twinkling stars and decided this would be the perfect setting for a romantic nighttime stroll. Plus, walking would take a little more time, and I was still in no rush to say goodnight to him.

"Let's walk."

"Sounds good to me," he agreed with a smile.

We continued to chat as we walked and were back at my car before I knew it. Mine was the only one left in the field, and as we got to it, my heart sank a little bit—knowing that our time together was now coming to an end.

"Thank you so much, Brayden," I said, turning to face him. "I had the best time with you today. Between making the snowman and sliding, I haven't had this much fun in a long time." I took his hands in mine as I continued, "And your surprise tonight was the sweetest thing anyone has ever done for me. You made me feel so special. Thirty-two is going in the books as my best birthday ever—and it's all because of you."

"You're welcome, Sunny. You deserve to feel special on your birthday," he said with a soft smile. He looked at my face in the moonlight for a second, then said, "I figured we're about the same age, but I know better than to ask a lady that question."

"So, when is your birthday?"

"I turned thirty-three back in October."

"Did you do anything exciting?"

He shook his head. "Just worked—which my mom and April yelled at me for. They get on me all the time for working too much. They're always trying to get me to take a day off." He sighed and said, "And today would have been no different. I was planning to work all day, and I would have felt awful for bailing on the kids. They begged me to build that snowman with them for weeks." A smile spread across his face. "I had so much fun today, and my first day off in a long time was even more worth it because of who I spent it with."

He took off one of his gloves and ran his fingers through my hair. "I wasn't sure what my mom was up to this morning when she texted me, but I'm really grateful she did. Little did I know what was waiting for me under that tent. Today might be your birthday, Sunny, but it's been a very special day for me too."

He held my gaze for a few seconds—then I watched as his focus slowly worked its way down my face. The rush of butterflies returned to my stomach, my heart racing as I imagined his lips on mine. He inched closer to me, and I didn't move—hoping the moment I'd been waiting for all day would finally happen. I closed my eyes, and I could feel his lips. They were soft, and his breath was warm...on my cheek. He gave me one last hug, and I opened my eyes as he straightened up.

A SUNNY DAY IN WINTER

"Goodnight, Sunny," he said as he opened my car door for me.

"Goodnight, Brayden."

I watched him in my rearview mirror as I was leaving. He remained standing in the field until I was out of sight.

I UNLOCKED THE DOOR to my apartment and was greeted by Ellie—meowing at me for her welcome-home cuddles. I picked her up, and she purred contentedly—listening to the details of my day while I got ready for bed.

It was just after midnight as I was settling under my covers. I picked up my phone to set the alarm and realized this was the first time I had touched it since handing it to Sam so he could take pictures of the four of us with our snowman.

I opened my photos, and my heart swelled as I looked at them. All of us were smiling at the camera—the kids looking so proud and excited. Sam had taken three pictures. The first two looked the same—but I had to catch my breath when I saw the last one. The kids and I stayed focused on the camera, but Brayden was looking at me. Now it made sense why Sam had quickly snapped one last picture of us and why he made the slight adjustment to the angle of my phone. More of Brayden's face was now visible—not just his side profile—and his features had completely changed in that split second. His expression went from someone who had won a competition to what looked like a man admiring the most beautiful woman he'd ever seen. His eyes had softened, and even though his smile wasn't as big, he looked even happier. Like he was content to stand there and be in my presence—not needing anything else but to be with me. All I could do was sit and stare at my phone, once again captivated by this man I had just met. Thinking back throughout the day and now looking at this picture gave me hope that he really does feel the same way I do. I was so grateful that Sam had taken this one last shot. He truly had captured the perfect moment in time.

As much as I wanted to keep looking at Brayden's handsome face, I knew I needed to get some sleep before my shift at the spa. So, I reluctantly set my alarm for 6:30, put my phone on my nightstand and switched out the light. Ellie came up to sleep on me as she usually did, and I relaxed to the sound of her purring. As I drifted to sleep, I felt such peace and contentment—knowing that today worked out exactly as it was supposed to.

Chapter 8

♥

"YOU SAID WHAT TO him?"

It was now Sunday evening, and I was at Allison's house. Since she had to dress professionally for work, she was in her typical weekend attire—jeans, and a flannel shirt, with her short brown hair tucked under a red baseball hat. I had worked my shift at the spa and stopped by to visit and catch her up on yesterday's happenings. And I wanted to check in on Zachary, who was feeling much better.

"And my voice sounded like a squeaky chicken."

Why was I telling her all this? I need to take a page out of Kyle's book and learn to keep my mouth shut. With every detail I gave her, I could see her getting increasingly annoyed with me. Her brown eyes were so huge that I was afraid they would pop right out of their sockets, and her jaw was practically on the floor. I could hear her thoughts about how I needed to listen to her, and I just knew the lecture was coming. So, before she could even start yelling at me, I went into full-on ramble mode—my voice super high-pitched and panicky.

"But it's okay because we built a snowman, we went sliding, and he surprised me with sandwiches, cake, candles, and flowers. Well, he didn't get me flowers, but he was able to save the ones that his niece and nephew knocked over. And we sat next to a fireplace, and he hung up our coats together, and he walked me back to my car in the moonlight at the end of the night, and—"

"Sunny, Sunny." She cut me off, reaching out and grabbing my hands. "Calm down."

I stopped talking and held my breath—not sure what to expect.

"He did all of that for you?"

I nodded and cautiously exhaled, hoping I might be off the hook from a scolding.

"Wow. He must be quite the guy to have your first encounter be like that and not go running for the hills."

I smiled and said, "He is so sweet, Allison. I've never met anyone like him."

She leaned in and hugged me. "I'm so happy for you, Sunny. You deserve to meet a great guy after everything you've been through."

"Thanks," I said to her as she let me go.

"So, what does he look like?"

I pulled out my phone and opened my pictures.

"Ooh la la—look at him," she said teasingly, wiggling her eyebrows at me. "So, these kids are his niece and nephew?"

"Yeah, they are so much like Russ and me, you wouldn't believe it."

"Another one of you? I didn't think that was possible!" she joked as she batted at my leg. "Your snowman is really creative. Whose idea was that?"

"The kids came up with it. Brayden gave them a little guidance and then left the rest to their imaginations."

"Aww, what a sweet uncle," she said, putting her hand over her heart. I watched as she swiped to the last picture—curious to see her reaction. She did a double take, then looked up at me—her eyes alight with happiness. "Sunny, he's smiling at you."

"I know." A warm feeling came over me as I thought about that picture and how it made me feel when I first saw it last night.

She was looking at my phone again as she said, "And his face looks different as he's looking at you. This guy really likes you, Sunny."

"So, you see it too?" I asked tentatively. "When I first saw that picture last night, I was surprised to see him looking at me—and I thought I noticed a change in his expression." I hesitated for a second, then added quietly, "So, it wasn't just me being my overly hopeful self?"

"No, Sunny, this time you're not being overly hopeful. Which is something we all love about you," she said with a gentle laugh. "And I'm guessing whoever took this picture noticed it too because they switched the camera angle to get a better view of his face."

"Yeah, that was his brother-in-law, Sam. It looked like he was done taking pictures of us, but then he snapped that last one really quick when he noticed Brayden looking at me."

She handed my phone back to me and said, "So when are you seeing him again?"

I stopped and thought for a second, not sure how to answer.

"You are seeing him again, right?" She raised her eyebrows at me expectantly.

I opened my mouth to try and give her a response, but her intense glare was making me nervous. I was worried I was about to be in trouble and unable to talk my way out of it this time.

"Did you at least get his phone number?"

"No," I said quietly, looking away from her.

"Sydney!"

Oh boy. Here we go.

"Have I taught you nothing in all the years we've been friends? You had a fantastic time with a charming guy—who, by the way, you squeaked at about your cat, in case I have to remind you—and he still stuck around, and you didn't even get his phone number?"

"Uh-oh. I heard a 'Sydney.'" Allison's boyfriend Nick entered the living room just then—a tall man with buzz-cut brown hair and blue eyes. Dressed in his typical t-shirt and shorts combo, he sat down in his chair with an amused grin. "What did the poor girl do this time, Allison?"

"Hi, Nick," I said to him with a slight smile.

"Sunny went to Chester yesterday and met an amazing man," Allison told him. "He spent the whole day with her, made a snowman, went sliding, and even planned a beautiful birthday surprise. All this after she squeaked at him about Ellie as soon as she met him." I could feel the daggers in her glare—still unable to look at her.

"Wow—all that after you admitted to the guy that you're a crazy cat lady?" Nick asked me.

I just nodded.

"Give me your phone," Allison demanded. I handed it over, and she showed Nick the picture of Brayden smiling at me. "Do you see the way he's looking at Sunny?"

His eyes landed on the picture, and his response was instant and full of conviction. "Wow! This guy has it bad for you, Sunny." He looked at me and held up my phone, so I could see the picture as he pointed at it. "A man doesn't look at just any woman like this."

"Thanks, Nick." Yet one more person gave me the validation I needed. And this time, it was coming from a man.

"So, what's the problem?" he asked Allison.

"She didn't set up another date or even get his phone number."

"How did you meet him?"

"He and his sister own the bakery we read about online," I replied.

"So just go back to the bakery," Nick stated plainly.

I looked at Allison and shrugged. "Yeah, that makes sense."

Nick chuckled at his girlfriend. "Lighten up, Allison. She's your best friend, not one of your employees."

She laughed and said, "Sunny probably wishes she was one of my employees since I'm nicer to them than I am to her most of the time." She sighed and took my hand. "You're the only person I'm this direct with, but it's because you're my best friend, and I want you to be happy."

I smiled at her. "I know. And just like how you love my eternal optimism, I love your directness. And it was because of your directness that I went to Chester yesterday—which led me to meet Brayden. So, I guess I should be thanking you."

She smiled at me and said, "You're welcome, Sunny. And now that we've gotten that all straightened out, when are you going back to the bakery?"

"I have tomorrow off from work. Do you think it would be okay if I stopped in to see him so soon?"

"Yes!" they both answered at the same time.

All three of us laughed, and Allison said, "Trust us, Sunny, this guy is into you. The sweet and quirky you. He knew in that first instant what he'd be getting himself into—and he still smiled at you like that and gave you a birthday to remember. You get back to that bakery tomorrow. He will be thrilled to see you again."

"Thanks, guys," I said, smiling at the two of them.

As usual, I felt perfect after talking to both of them. Allison is always the voice of not-so-subtle reason, and Nick helps to buffer her directness. I left their place and headed home, optimistic about what tomorrow will bring.

Chapter 9

I ARRIVED IN CHESTER the following day feeling cute and stylish in a light pink sweater, skinny jeans, and knee-high brown boots. Instead of loose curls, I straightened my hair and opted for my large, bold glasses instead of contacts. The only thing that doesn't change about my look is how I do my makeup. It's always light and natural, just enough to enhance my features and make me feel girly.

With Allison and Nick's voices echoing in my head, I confidently opened the door to the bakery and stepped inside, excited to see Brayden again but slightly nervous. Since we hadn't traded phone numbers, I knew it was up to me to make the next move, and I was hoping he would be happy to see me. As it turns out, there was no need for me to be anxious because as soon as I entered the bakery, I was literally greeted with open arms.

"Sunny! You're back!" April's eyes brightened as she came out from behind the counter and hugged me.

"Happy belated birthday," she said as she let me go. "I knew I couldn't say anything two days ago without spoiling my brother's surprise."

"Thanks, April," I said, smiling at her. "Brayden's surprise was the sweetest thing anyone has ever done for me."

"As I was pushing you through the kitchen door, I caught a glimpse of what he had done, and it looked so romantic in here. I didn't know my brother had it in him," she said as she slipped her arm into mine and led me to the counter.

Marissa came out of the kitchen and smiled from ear to ear when she saw me, and I found myself in another cheerful embrace. "Happy birthday, two days late! I was getting ready to lock the door when Brayden showed up the other day and told me what he had planned. I asked him if he needed help, but he said he was all set and had gotten a temporary pass into the kitchen."

"When he told me what he wanted to do, I was so happy for the two of you, I didn't hesitate—figuring he couldn't make too much of a mess," April said with a little laugh. "I have to admit, though, I was a little nervous as I unlocked the door yesterday morning, but there was no evidence that he had even been in the kitchen."

"Speaking of messes your brother makes"—Marissa handed April a note—"he left this for me. I've gotten pretty good at reading his handwriting over the past three years, but this time it's completely illegible. I cannot figure out what he is trying to say."

"Wow! You're right. It is worse than usual," April said, straining to make sense of his writing. Then she looked at me and said, "Besides being banished from the kitchen, my brother is also not allowed to write on these chalk-boards."

She showed me the note, and after I had studied it for a moment, I said, "Your brother's handwriting is...interesting." I was being nice. It was horrible. "It looks like it says, 'Marissa, I need your hours from last week. Thanks, Brayden.'"

The two of them looked at the note again. Then they looked at each other, and Marissa said, "She gets Mr. Serious to smile and be romantic—and she can read his writing? We need this girl to stick around!" She gave me a quick smile, then she turned and headed back into the kitchen.

"Would you like something to eat, Sunny?" April asked me.

It was still a little too early for lunch, and since I arrived later today than I did on Saturday, several of the pastries were gone by now. There were still a few muffins, so I ordered a blueberry one and a cup of coffee. I got out my wallet, and April held up a hand and responded, "It's on the house."

"Thanks, April," I said to her, appreciating the kind gesture.

"It's the least I can do, Sunny. You brought out a whole new side of my brother two days ago that we weren't sure we would ever see. We should be thanking you." She smiled at me and said, "Go have a seat. I'll warm up your muffin and bring everything over to you in a minute."

I picked up my bag and went to one of the tables in the middle of the room. As much as I loved the table next to the fireplace, I didn't want to sit there without Brayden. It wouldn't be as special without him. Plus, this table gave me a bird's eye view of the place, including the door. It didn't seem like Brayden was here, and if he showed up, I wanted to be the first to see. I took off my coat and scarf and draped them over my chair, and I found myself in another hug before I could sit down—this time from Lauren.

"Happy birthday, Sunny!"

"Thanks, Lauren." I smiled at her as she let me go.

"As soon as April got back in the car the other day, she told us why we had to get here so fast. At least then the bossy pants made sense," she said with a little laugh.

I took her hands and said, "Your son is the sweetest man I have ever met. He made my birthday truly special and unforgettable and was a perfect gentleman the entire time."

Her eyes brightened up at my compliment on her son. "I'm so happy to hear that, Sunny," she said, giving my hands a thankful squeeze. "His father and I are really proud of him."

As she said that, I realized this was the first mention of his dad, whom I still haven't met.

A moment later, April showed up at the table holding a tray with my muffin, a cinnamon roll, and two coffees.

She set everything down and said, "Do you mind if I join you for a little bit? We had a busy morning, and I could use a break."

"Sure, I would love the company," I beamed, delighted to have a new friend.

We sat across from each other as Lauren went back up front to take care of a few things. Once again, I felt very welcome in their bakery—like I belonged as part of their family.

"So, you had a nice time with Brayden on Saturday?" April asked me as we were enjoying our treats.

"I did. The entire day was amazing, but that surprise of his was incredible. The way he decorated this place with candles and rose petals brought tears to my eyes. And thanks for giving him a pass into the kitchen," I said with a little laugh. "He said the sandwiches weren't much, but they were a lot to me. I don't need grand gestures. The little moments in life, the small acts of kindness—that's what really matters. The way your brother treated me the whole day—especially once we were back here—made me feel so special and cared for."

"That's because he really does care about you, Sunny. I have never seen my brother look at anyone like how he looks at you." She paused for a second, then said, "I'm guessing you've seen the pictures Sam took of the four of you with the snowman. Especially that last one."

"Yeah, I looked at them as I was getting into bed Saturday night. I noticed his face had changed when he was looking at me. I stopped in to see my friend Allison last night, and she and her boyfriend Nick also saw it. They told me I needed to come back to the bakery—that I wasn't just being hopeful and that he would want to see me again."

"Is she the friend you were supposed to come to the carnival with?"

I nodded.

"How is her son feeling?"

"He's much better, thanks," I told her.

"I'm happy to hear that," she said with a smile, then she was quiet for a second before continuing. "But if I'm being honest, I'm actually glad that your friends weren't able to come with you the other day. This way, we got you all to ourselves—especially Brayden. Something changed in his eyes right in that first moment he saw you. Mom and I both noticed it." She looked down at her coffee cup for a second, then back up at me. "But the part that totally shocked us was when you told him about your cat."

I put my face in my hands and shook my head. "Not my best moment April. I still can't believe I did that."

"No, Sunny, you don't understand." She put her hand on my arm, and I looked up at her. "You didn't see it because you were busy restacking the coffee cups, but as soon as he noticed you getting all flustered, his entire demeanor changed."

"How so?"

"His face suddenly lit up in a smile. A genuine smile. And it was great to see because it's something that hasn't happened much these last few years."

"Really?" I asked her. "I've had guys laugh at my quirkiness before, but it's usually followed by an eye roll and them running for the hills."

She shook her head. "My brother wasn't laughing at you, Sunny. In fact, it was just the opposite. It was like a switch turned on, and he became alive again. Brayden's always been rather serious. It's just who he is. That's why I tease him so much, trying to get him to lighten up. But all it took was one moment with you, and Mr. Serious started to disappear, replaced by someone else. There were times I didn't even recognize him the other day, like his reaction to me messing up his spreadsheet. He was totally different."

"What do you mean?"

"I don't usually touch his computer, knowing how hard he works. But when Sam brought the kids back after the snowman competition, he said he had been watching the two of you, and it looked like Brayden was actually having fun for once. Then when he told me about the picture he took of my brother smiling at you and the look on his face, I could not have been happier for him. So, I figured I would take a little bit of the work off his plate and help him, but when the screen went blank, I panicked. Marissa told me he was in the bakery, so I ran to find him, only to interrupt the two of you having lunch in the most romantic spot in the whole place. Sorry about that," she said with an apologetic smile.

"It's okay," I told her. "Watching the two of you together was quite entertaining."

We shared a laugh, then she continued, "Anyway, the part that really surprised me about Brayden's reaction was when he said, 'It's just a spreadsheet.' The man is obsessed with his spreadsheets and keeping them accurate. That's why I knew I had to pull out the 'Brady,' figuring he would be mad at me. So, when I got the opposite reaction, all I could do was stare at him and wonder who he was and what he did with my brother. It's like he's a completely different man since he met you. And I mean that in a good way, you are definitely bringing out the best in him." She reached across the table, squeezed my hand, and said, "Mom and I are so happy that you came back. And your friends were right. Brayden will be too."

Just then, the door opened, and my heart leaped into my throat as I heard a masculine voice say, "Okay, Mom. What's the big emergency this time?"

Brayden walked up to the counter where Lauren was standing, and I heard her say, "Look who's here."

He turned around and scanned the room. As soon as his focus landed on me, his face instantly brightened. He smiled at me, and I stood up as he walked over to our table, his eyes staying on mine the entire time.

"Hi, Sunny," he said, hugging me. I breathed in his scent; the fresh, woodsy smell was more prominent this time. I delighted in his embrace for a long moment—realizing how much I missed being in his arms, how natural and comfortable he felt. I could tell from the look on his face and how he was hugging me that he was pleased to see me again.

"Hi, Brayden." I smiled at him after he let me go and took in his appearance. This time he was dressed much more casually. He was still wearing jeans but had them paired with a red and gray plaid flannel shirt and a dark blue vest. He had some sawdust on his clothes and hair, and I'm guessing he hadn't shaved since Saturday morning because he had a few days' facial hair growth. He looked handsome both ways, but I agree with Vicki. The clean-shaven face made him look a bit younger.

April was now standing, looking at her brother with her arms crossed. "You're lucky she came back." Then she turned to me and said, "I yelled at him for not getting your phone number." Her eyes returned to Brayden, and she scanned his outfit with disapproval. "But it looks like I should have told you to shave and dress nicely again."

He thought for a second, then said, "Those texts were from you? I thought they were from Mom."

"Would you have taken them seriously if I had sent them from my phone?"

"Probably not," he admitted.

She gave him a satisfied smile and said, "You're welcome." Then, she picked up our empty plates and headed to the kitchen.

Brayden and I sat down as I said to him, "So your sister yelled at you?"

"She did," he said with a sigh.

"So did my best friend. She even called me 'Sydney.'"

"Ouch! But at least you didn't get a 'Sydney Michaela,'" he said with a playful smile. "Which is basically what my sister did to me. But whenever she calls me by my full name, I just remind her who she sounds like, and that gets her off my back."

"And thankfully, I have Allison's boyfriend, Nick, on my side. He came to my defense, telling me to just come back to the bakery."

"I'm glad you did. It's great to see you again, Sunny." He looked at me quietly, his eyes sparkling as he added, "And you look really pretty in your glasses."

"Thanks, Brayden."

I couldn't help but smile, knowing he was genuinely happy that I had returned. April gave me the same validation as Allison and Nick, and now I was getting first-hand confirmation from the man himself. I breathed a sigh of relief that my eternal optimism was for real this time, and I relaxed as we continued to have a good time getting to know one another.

WE HAD BEEN SITTING there for quite a while and had just placed our orders for lunch when the door opened, and a female voice said, "Hey pretty girl, I'll take a mocha latte to go."

Brayden's body language instantly changed. His posture got more rigid, and his eyes were huge with panic, darting around frantically, looking for a way to escape. He recognized the voice; it was Vicki. I knew I needed to help him, so I reached across the table and took his hands in mine, hoping that if she saw us together, she would lighten up her flirtations. As soon as my hands touched his, everything about him relaxed—his posture as well as his face. His eyes calmed down as they met mine, and he smiled with a sense of relief. And I was just in time, too, because Vicki seemed to have radar that honed in on his presence.

"Brayden," she said, sauntering over to us, her eyes once again scanning him. "I see you're going for the rugged outdoorsman look today. I like it."

She reached out and touched his shoulder, making his eyes snap shut as he inhaled a sharp breath, and I could feel the cringe he was trying so hard to suppress politely. I knew I needed to make this look more convincing, so I adjusted our hands, intertwining our fingers. And with that one simple change, everything felt different. I wasn't just saving him from an overzealous cougar anymore. Now it felt like we were an actual couple. I got the sense he felt it, too, because he gently caressed my fingers as he exhaled all the air he was holding, his eyes calm as they opened to meet mine.

"Hi Vicki," he said to her, his eyes not leaving mine. "You remember Sunny from the snowman competition, right?"

I looked at her and smiled. "Hi Vicki, it's nice to see you again."

"It's nice to see you too, hon," she said, smiling at me—then her face fell as she noticed our hands on the table. She dropped her hand, and I could feel the gratitude in the gentle squeeze he gave my fingers.

"Brayden and I had the best time together on Saturday, and I just had to come back to the bakery and see him again." I looked at him and smiled. "After spending the whole day having fun outside, he gave me the most romantic birthday surprise that lasted well into the night."

"Wasn't that nice of him," she said, with a tone that was a mixture of sarcasm and jealousy. I looked back at her and based on her expression; I think she was finally getting the hint that he wasn't interested in her.

Marissa showed up next to us with a cup in her hand. "Here you go, Vicki."

"Thanks, dear," she said with a half-hearted smile, then she made her way to the door as April arrived at our table with two plates and two glasses of water.

"What's this now?" she said, looking down at our hands—fingers still interlocked.

"This is Sunny saving your brother from Vicki," Marissa said to her.

"And she really did save me, too," Brayden said as we pulled our hands apart so April could set our plates and glasses down. "Do you think she bought it?"

As Marissa turned around to head back to the kitchen, she leaned into April and said, "I've been buying it since these two walked in here together on Saturday."

"I have something else for you, too," April said as she finished putting our lunch in front of us. "Here's your flowers from the other day." She picked up the vase of pink and white carnations and placed our pink tulips in the middle of the table.

"Thanks, April," I said, my eyes brightening as I looked at the tulips. I loved that she referred to them as 'our flowers.' It made me feel overjoyed—knowing Brayden and I already had something special and unique to the two of us. I got the impression that he felt the same way when I looked up at him and noticed his eyes shining as well.

OUR LUNCH WAS FINISHED, and we were cozy in each other's company when the door opened again. This time, it was Lauren and the kids.

Hurricane Cassidy came rushing over to our table, excited to tell us all about her day at school. As usual, her brother was in tow, letting his sister do all the talking. Brayden pushed his chair back and pulled her onto his lap, smiling at me across the table as we listened to her talk for a solid ten minutes. Kyle was apparently getting bored just standing there listening to his sister and decided to pull up a nearby chair and sit next to me.

"How was your day at school, Kyle?" I was finally able to ask when his sister stopped talking long enough to drink some of Brayden's water.

"Good," he replied quietly.

"Uncle Brayden," Cassidy was back to chatting again. "You're coming to our house tonight, right?"

"Of course," he said to her. Then he turned his attention to me, his smile growing extensive. "Sunny, if you're free tonight, you're welcome to join us. We do pizza and a movie every Monday night."

My expression mirrored his, so happy for the invitation. "Thanks, Brayden, that sounds like fun."

April appeared at our table, and Cassidy said excitedly, "Mommy, Sunny's coming over tonight!" She jumped off Brayden's lap, came over, and hugged me, then she and Kyle ran into the kitchen to tell Lauren about their dinner guest.

"Great!" April said, her eyes full of optimism as she looked at me. "Hopefully, with you there, my brother won't just work the entire time."

"What are we watching tonight?" he asked, ignoring her last comment.

"Ice Age, the original one. We'll be locking up here soon, and you can follow us to my place, Sunny." Then she turned to her brother and wagged her finger at him. "And no working tonight!"

"The work never stops when you own a business April."

She put her hands on her hips, gave him a severe look, and said, "Brayden Alexander Mont—" She cut herself off when she noticed the change in her brother's expression.

He was pointing at her with a stern look that seemed only half serious—like there was an inside joke between them.

"Don't make me say it." His raised eyebrows gave way to the grin slowly spreading over his face.

A SUNNY DAY IN WINTER

She stared at him for a second, and then her face lit up into a smile as she said, "Don't make me get Vicki back in here." They both laughed as she teasingly swatted her brother on the shoulder with the towel she was holding.

Yet again, I found myself amused by their sibling banter.

Chapter 10

♥

I FOLLOWED EVERYONE TO April's place, one of the old stone houses on Route 103 that the Chester Depot Village is famous for. Ideal for a family—complete with a large maple tree out front, providing the perfect spot for a tire swing for the kids. The house is two stories, with large stones of varying sizes and shades of brown and gray, set with mortar the color of a sandy beach. A glass front door and several white-trimmed windows let in plenty of natural light. Much of the old charm is still intact in the kitchen and living room—with wooden beams running along the ceilings, original hardwood floors, and a large stone fireplace in the living room.

I offered to help the ladies make the pizzas, to which Lauren replied with a smile, "No, Sunny, you're our guest for the evening."

"And Marissa told me about your bread, so I think we need to banish you from the kitchen too," April said good-naturedly. "Besides, you're the only reason why this one here isn't sitting at the table glued to his computer right now." She stared at her brother with her arms crossed, her raised eyebrows challenging him to deny her accusation.

Cassidy unknowingly helped him out of April's criticizing glare when she grabbed his hand and said, "Uncle Brayden, you and Sunny have to come play with us."

"Come on, Sunny," he said, taking my hand and leading me toward the living room. "Let's go where we're wanted." He smiled at his sister in friendly surrender as her face relaxed into a satisfied grin.

We chased the kids around for a while until Lauren told us dinner was ready. Just as we returned to the kitchen, the door opened, and Sam walked in, home from work.

"Sunny! It's so nice to see you again," he said.

"Hi Sam," I replied.

He went over to April, kissed her hello, and said, "I told you she'd be back. There was no need to yell at your brother yesterday."

"There's always a need for me to yell at my brother," she said, playfully swatting at Brayden again.

The seven of us sat around the table, enjoying our pizza and chatting about our day. It was nice to feel like a part of the family, and it reminded me of eating dinner with Russ and my parents growing up.

After dinner, April and Lauren stood up to clear the table and again declined my offer to help.

"You and Brayden, go make yourselves comfortable in the living room. This will only take us a few minutes," April said, ushering us out of the kitchen.

The living room was set up with a large, light gray sectional and two chairs arranged in a horseshoe, with several bright, colorful throw pillows and blankets adding vibrant pops of color, and a dark blue area rug covered the wide-plank hardwood floor. A large coffee table and two end tables were scattered amongst the furniture, and a tv-stand with glass doors sat next to the fireplace—all made from maple. They were beautifully crafted, and I guessed they were handmade upon closer look. Before we sat down to dinner, the guys had built a fire, and Brayden added a few more logs as we came in. An impressive mantle matched the beams on the ceiling, lined with pictures and a few winter-themed decorations. Just like at the bakery, it made for a very romantic atmosphere.

I sat across from the fireplace and watched him, quietly enjoying our first few moments of privacy. When he finished, he sat down facing me and took my hands in his, intertwining our fingers. It took me back to that moment we shared in the bakery, but my feelings were even stronger now. My heart swelled with joy since, this time, he was the one who initiated it.

"Movie night will be so much better with you here, Sunny. My sister was right, I usually work through the entire movie, and tonight would have been no exception. I don't have the heart to tell her this, but I couldn't save the spreadsheet that she messed up. I had to start all over, and

I need it for an important meeting on Wednesday." Then he smiled at me and said, "But Mr. Serious has tomorrow to worry about that. Thanks for coming over tonight and giving me something more important to focus on."

"Thanks for inviting me, Brayden," I said, smiling as I shifted my gaze to our hands.

His fingers gently stroked mine as he spoke. "When you held my hands like this at the bakery earlier, the whole world disappeared—even Vicki. In a split second, I went from feeling like I was being saved from a cougar to feeling like I was part of a couple." He took one of his hands and tilted my chin up, and as my eyes met his, he added quietly, "And I know you felt it too." He held my gaze as he tilted his head to the side, a gentle smile on his face.

Our intimate moment was interrupted as his family started coming into the room. April and Lauren set bowls of popcorn on the coffee table, and everyone claimed their spots for the evening.

I grabbed a large turquoise pillow, tossed it on the floor in front of me, and turned to Brayden. "Come here. I'll rub your neck and shoulders while we watch the movie."

His eyes lit up. "Thanks, Sunny." He sat down on the pillow and leaned back against my legs that were crossed up on the couch. The tension melted from his shoulders as soon as my hands started. "Mmm," he sighed content-edly. "That feels amazing."

Sam was the last to come in, and he did a double-take when he noticed us. "No computer tonight, Brayden?"

"Left it at home," he said, closing his eyes and letting out a contented sigh.

Sam was still looking curiously at Brayden as he sat next to April and said, "What is happening to Mr. Serious?" She looked over at us and smiled as she snuggled up next to her husband.

We were about an hour into the movie when Sam got up to get more popcorn from the kitchen. When he returned to the living room, he looked at Brayden, then said to April, "What's with your brother?"

"What do you mean?"

"Look at him. It looks like he's sleeping. I've never seen him so relaxed."

The three of them looked at me and smiled, then Lauren quietly said to April, "Since he is so relaxed, right now might be a good time to tell him about the bank."

"Tell me what about the bank, Mom?" Brayden asked.

"Oh, you heard that?"

"Of course, I heard that." Then he looked up at me and said, "My family forgets that I have Vulcan hearing." He leaned his head against my knee and looked at his sister. "So, you need to tell me something?"

She looked nervous, and since his head was turned to the side, I switched to raking my fingers through his hair.

"Um, Brady?" she said, fidgeting with her rings again.

"What now, April?" he sighed.

"You know how you have that meeting with the guy from the bank on Wednesday, right?"

"Mm-hmm," he said lazily, closing his eyes.

"Well, he needed to push up your appointment time, and I told him it was okay."

"And you figured this would upset me; why?"

"Because he's meeting you at the bakery at seven-thirty," she quickly confessed.

His eyes popped open wide at hearing her admission.

"That's why I waited so long to tell you."

"When did he switch the time?"

"A week ago." Her response was barely a squeak.

"So why are you waiting until now to tell me?"

"Because I didn't want to listen to you complain for a whole week about how you would have to get up early."

He opened his mouth to reply, then stopped. I'm guessing because he knew she was right. His expression relaxed, and he calmly said, "Like I'm always telling you—it's what you do when you own a business. I guess I need to take my own advice." Then he closed his eyes again and leaned back against my legs, moving my hands to resume working on his shoulders.

April stopped fidgeting with her rings, her hands dropping heavily in her lap. She stared at her brother in stunned silence, her mouth gaping open. Then a smile slowly spread across her face as she lifted her eyes to me. "Marissa's right, Sunny. We really do need to keep you around!"

Brayden reached up and gave my hands a gentle squeeze of agreement.

"Is everything okay with the bakery?" she asked her brother.

"Yes, April, everything is okay with the bakery."

"The guy you're meeting with is the Vice President, right?"

"It's not a big deal—half the employees in a bank are 'Vice Presidents,'" he said, using air quotes. "And remember, the financial stuff is mine to worry about." He gave his sister a reassuring smile, and she relaxed—knowing everything was okay with the bakery and her business partner.

Sam chimed back in with a mischievous grin on his face. "And if things don't work out with the bank, I know someone who's offered to be an investor." Brayden's shoulders tensed up, and I had a feeling why. "I'm sure the Vickster has a long list of creative payment options for you to choose from," he teased his brother-in-law, wiggling his eyebrows.

I felt Brayden shudder. "There is no way I'm selling my soul to that woman."

"She clearly makes you uncomfortable. Why don't you tell her to go pound sand?"

"Because Alex and I raised him to be polite," Lauren said, smiling at her son.

"And I know she's not a bad person. I just wish she would stop hitting on me," he said with a sigh.

"Sunny rescued Brayden earlier today," April said to Sam and Lauren. "Vicki stopped by, and Sunny held his hands like they were a couple—interlocked fingers and everything. They looked so natural and believable." Then she smiled at me and said, "It's one more reason we're happy to have you around."

Brayden reached up and slid his fingers between mine, resting our hands together on his shoulders. I gently stroked his neck with my thumbs as he looked up at me and smiled. A warmth of contentment spread through me as I saw my feelings mirrored in his eyes. What seemed like a simple gesture to everyone else had a secret, special meaning exclusive to the two of us.

AFTER THE MOVIE, THE kids hugged us goodnight, and Sam and Lauren took them to get ready for bed while April, Brayden, and I took the empty popcorn bowls to the kitchen.

"If you're free on Wednesday, you should stop by the bakery," April said to me. "You can see my brother all dressed up and acting like a big-shot business owner. He puts on a suit, and he goes from Mr. Serious to Mr. Executive, talking about budgets and statistics. Or something boring like that, I don't really pay attention to him."

"That's why I do these meetings by myself and catch my sister up afterward," Brayden said to me, glancing sideways at April.

"Yeah, but I still don't listen. Baking is the fun part." She playfully poked at her brother as she said, "But maybe Sunny will find your fancy math sexy." She stepped closer to me and said, "If you're lucky, he might even show you his...*spreadsheets*." She whispered that last word in my ear in a seductive voice that made me laugh at the good-natured way she picked on her brother.

"I don't know about you, April," he said, shaking his head and laughing. Then he grabbed our coats and said, "Come on, Sunny, I'll walk you to your car before my sister digs herself in any deeper."

We stepped outside into the quiet freshness, the moonlit sky setting a romantic atmosphere. He took my hand, and we slowly walked over to my car. Turning to face me, he ran his fingers through my hair, tucking it behind my ear. I looked up at his handsome features, his irresistible smile glowing in the darkness.

"You don't know how happy I was to see you sitting in the bakery today. I couldn't stop thinking about you yesterday, and I was hoping you would come back."

"I thought about you all day yesterday, too," I confessed in agreement, my eyes not leaving his. "I asked Nick and Allison if they thought I should come back today, hoping it wouldn't be too soon. I didn't want to wait any longer to see you again."

"You could have come back yesterday," he assured me, his voice sounding so deep and sexy. "That's how bad I wanted to see you."

He stepped closer to me, and I knew his precise intentions as I followed his blue eyes down to my lips. My heart sped up as his face slowly inched toward mine—a man in no rush—intensifying every part of this moment. I must admit, as much as I craved to feel his kiss, the build-up of anticipation made it even more exciting. My eyes drifted shut as his face lingered right in front of mine, his warm breath teasing me in the cold night air...

...creak...

"Samuel!" April's voice shrieked from withinside the house.

"What?" he said innocently. "I'm taking out the trash. Without even being asked this time, I might add."

"Get back in here! You can do that in a minute!"

The romance officially gone; I opened my eyes and met Brayden's, his obvious disappointment mirroring mine. We looked over at Sam, whose now pale face stared at the two of us as if he had just accidentally walked in on someone in the bathroom.

"I saw nothing..." he sheepishly uttered before slinking back inside, the trash bag still clutched in his right hand.

Even as the door creaked shut, I could hear April inside reading Sam the riot act.

Brayden shook his head and said, "I'm sorry about my sister. Besides being bossy, she's also nosy."

"It's okay," I said with a small laugh. "I feel kind of bad for Sam though."

"He'll be fine," he said with a slight chuckle. "Yelling at us is just what she does." His face relaxed as he looked at me, the brightness returning to his eyes. "So, would you like to come by the bakery Wednesday?"

"Well, I hear Mr. Executive is making an appearance." I gave him a playful smile as I tugged at the collar on his coat. "There's no way I can miss that."

"And since my helpful secretary moved up my appointment, I should be done with the bank by eleven." He wrapped his hands around mine and tilted his head as he looked at me for a long moment, his eyes shining in the moonlight. "At least now, the rest of my day will be free because I'm already looking forward to seeing you again, Sunny."

"Me too, Brayden."

He hugged me good night, and I turned toward my car. Just then, I noticed out of the corner of my eye two familiar faces peeking through the kitchen window. I looked straight at them with an amused grin—and Lauren and April realized they were busted. Their faces quickly disappeared—the curtains snapping shut.

As I drove home, I felt so good about how today had gone. Brayden was genuinely happy to see me again, and we both felt our connection deepening.

Now, if only that kiss could happen...

Chapter 11

♥

Tuesday came and went, with my shift at the spa turning into a fun night dancing at Zumba class. Every time I imagined Brayden in his suit, I felt as giddy as a schoolgirl, daydreaming about the cute boy I had a crush on. Now that it was finally Wednesday morning, I was excitedly getting ready to head to Chester when my phone rang.

"Hi, Mom," I answered with a smile.

"Hi, Sunny. Did you and Allison have fun at the carnival on Saturday?"

Her question made me realize that I hadn't spoken to her or my dad since the morning of my birthday.

"Allison wasn't able to go. Zachary woke up sick."

"The poor little guy. Is he okay?"

"Yeah, he's fine now. I stopped in to see them on Sunday."

"So, if you didn't go to the carnival, what did you do instead?"

"I still went to the carnival, just by myself," I told her, feeling proud of myself for having the courage to go alone.

"You should have called us Sunny. Your dad and I didn't want you spending your birthday alone." I could tell by her voice that she felt terrible.

"Actually, I wasn't alone. I met a really nice family who invited me to spend the day with them."

"What's his name, Sunny?"

I love how my mom can always pick up on things just by how I sound. And I'm happy that it's so obvious.

"Brayden." A big smile spread across my face as I said his name.

"And how did you meet Brayden?"

"I went to the bakery Allison and I read about online. He owns it with his sister."

"So you got your cake, good."

"That came at the very end of the night. After spending the day with his family, he surprised me with a little celebration, just the two of us."

"Oh, Sunny!" I could hear the joy in her voice. "I'm so happy for you."

"Yeah, he's such a sweet guy. He's not like anyone I've ever met before." I paused for a second before adding, "Especially you know who."

"Good. One of him was more than enough," she said, her voice sounding more serious. "You deserve a great man after what he put you through."

"Thanks, Mom. I know."

"Have you told Brayden about him yet?"

"No, I've been waiting for the right time to bring it up. It's not exactly first date conversation material."

"That's true. I guess you'll know when the time is right."

"We've gotten together twice already, and we're seeing each other again today. I was getting ready when you called."

The cheeriness returned to her voice as she said, "Well then, I'll let you go so you can finish getting ready. Have fun, and I'll tell your dad the good news. And I mean it, Sunny. You really do deserve a great man."

"Thanks, Mom. I love you."

"I love you too, Sunny."

I smiled as I hung up, knowing how happy my mom was for me. My parents have always supported me, and I know they want me to find a man who will treat me right.

And I've found him.

I went back to getting ready when my phone rang again. This time it was Allison.

"Hey, beautiful!" I was so excited to catch up with her about Monday.

"Hi, Sunny. I'm in between meetings and figured I would quickly call you. How did it go on Monday?"

"Even better than I was hoping. You and Nick were right. He was thrilled to see me. He even invited me to his sister's house for their weekly movie night."

"That's great Sunny. I'm so excited for you." I could hear her talking to someone in the background for a second; then, she was back. "So was his dad at movie night?"

"No, I still haven't met him yet. His mom made a few quick references to him, but all I know so far is that his name is Alex. I figured when Brayden's ready; he'll introduce me to him."

"Yeah, I'm sure he will." I could hear her typing in the background. I know how demanding her job is, and I'm delighted she took the time to call me. "Now for the real reason I'm calling." I could tell just by the tone in her voice what her next question would be.

"No, he hasn't kissed me yet," I said with a sigh. "He was going to as we were saying goodnight, but his brother-in-law walked in on us."

"I knew it, Sunny! I knew he wanted to kiss you just by looking at that picture. It was written all over his face. So when are you seeing him again?"

"Today."

I could hear voices in the background again, and she said, "I'm sorry, but I have to go now; my meeting is starting. I really hope it happens for you this time; just make sure you're somewhere nice and private." Then she hung up before I got the chance to say anything else.

I smiled again as I looked at my phone. My heart was so full of love for my mom and Allison, both genuinely happy to hear my good news.

I was on cloud nine as I finished getting ready and headed out the door, excited for wherever today would bring me.

A SUNNY DAY IN WINTER

I walked into the bakery and looked around. There was no sign of Brayden yet, but April was behind the counter and noticed me come in.

"Sunny!" she said brightly. "I'm glad you decided to come." She came over and hugged me. "Brayden's meeting started here, and then they left to go to the bank. He should be back soon. Would you like something to eat while you wait?"

"Not yet, thanks. This way, I can have lunch with your brother when he returns. But I'll take a cup of coffee in the meantime."

"Sure, have a seat."

I took off my coat and sat down, and April appeared a minute later carrying two cups of coffee. She sat across from me, and like last time, I enjoyed her company while I waited for Brayden.

"I'm happy you joined us for movie night."

"Thanks, I had a great time. It was so sweet of your brother to invite me."

"I was so proud of him for leaving his computer at home; he's so focused on this place all the time. But I guess he's never had a good reason to set his work aside." She smiled at me as she said, "Until he met you. Mom and I have even tried fixing him up on dates, but he would always refuse, saying he was too busy." Then she added quickly, "Age-appropriate dates. I only threaten him with Vicki when he's annoying me. I wouldn't actually do that to him."

We both laughed, then she got quiet for a second. She looked down at her coffee cup and said, "I'm sorry Sam interrupted you two the other night. I didn't realize he was heading out the door until it was too late."

"It's okay, April," I said, reaching across the table and reassuringly squeezing her hand. "It'll happen when the time is right."

She looked up at me and breathed a sigh of relief, the brightness returning to her eyes. "I know. I just see how happy my brother is around you and how he looks at you. I'll make sure not to take up too much of his time when he gets done with his meeting today. I'll pretend to lose interest in what he's telling me even quicker than usual. And I lose interest pretty quickly as it is. I can only take so much of listening to his five-year plan and him constantly telling me, 'It's not in the budget, April.'" I laughed at her mocking facial expressions and tone of voice.

"It always amuses me, April, the way you—"

I stopped talking when the door opened, and Brayden walked in with another gentleman. Sure enough, he was dressed in a suit—but not just any suit you would pick up in a department store. His meticulously tailored charcoal gray jacket and pants hugged his body in all the right places. A silver tie rested on top of a light-blue shirt with French cuffs, silver cufflinks sparkling at his wrists. My scan finished on his perfectly polished black shoes—immaculate despite all the snow and salt out-side. His handsome face was freshly shaven, and his dark hair was combed neatly, not one strand out of place. I watched—mesmerized, as he went to a table across the room, sat with his business associate, and took out his computer. Seeing the cover on his laptop pulled me from my trance, and a chuckle escaped me. Even though he looked very distinguished and professional, the frosted donuts with sprinkles made Mr. Serious look fun and easygoing.

"Wow, April," I breathed. "Look at your brother." My wide eyes were still focused on him.

"Yeah, I figured you would want to see him all dressed up." I tore my attention away from him to see her smiling at me. "You're welcome."

APRIL AND I CONTINUED chatting while Brayden was in his meeting. At one point, the two of them got up and went into the kitchen, and he caught my eye as he walked by. He gave me a quick smile, then shifted his focus back to his conversation. Upon returning to their table, the other man picked up his belongings and turned to leave. Brayden walked him to the door, and as they shook hands goodbye, his associate said, "It was nice meeting you, Mr. Montgomery. You have a good day."

"Ooh, Mr. Montgomery. Don't you sound all fancy and important," April teased her brother when he came over to our table.

"Hi, Sunny," he said, bending down to hug me, ignoring his sister.

"Hi, Brayden," I replied, enjoying his quick embrace.

"Who was that guy?" April asked him. "He's different from the one you were talking to earlier."

Brayden had collected his materials from his meeting and was sorting through everything when he replied casually, "The bank's lawyer."

"Why were you meeting with their lawyer? What's going on?" Her eyes were huge with concern.

"Standard stuff April," he said as he tucked papers into his laptop case. "My part in running the business isn't just budgets and statistics." He raised his eyebrows as he looked at his sister. "It's also about networking and building relationships."

Brayden turned his attention to me just as she picked up one of his notepads and started browsing through it. "I'll catch my sister up on a few things and change my clothes. Then I'll be back." He noticed April looking at his notepad and snatched it from her hands. "And I'll put these in my car, so my sister can't snoop at my notes."

"Yeah, like I can read it anyway," she muttered, rolling her eyes. Then her face lit up as she looked at me and said, "Ooh, but Sunny can! She'll translate for me."

Brayden shook his head good-naturedly as he turned his sister toward the kitchen and said, "Come on, let's get this over with."

As they started to walk off, she stopped and faced me. "I'll have Marissa put lunch together for you two while we're chatting. What would you like?"

"A couple of 'Braydens?'" I suggested, smiling at him.

"Sounds good," he agreed, returning my smile.

AS PROMISED, APRIL WAS done with her brother in no time. Dressed in jeans, Brayden emerged from the kitchen folding the collar of his button-down shirt over the neck of a cable-knit gray sweater. Looking much more comfortable in his casual clothes, he came over and sat across from me.

Marissa appeared a moment later, carrying our lunch. As she set down our plates, she looked back and forth between us and said, "Did you two plan this?"

"Plan what?" he asked her.

"You're wearing matching sweaters today."

I looked down and realized she was right. I had chosen a gray and white marled sweater this morning.

"No, it's just a happy accident," I said, smiling at Brayden.

We enjoyed our lunch together and spent the early afternoon chatting until the bakery was getting ready to close. After clearing all the rest of the tables, Marissa said goodbye to us and headed out the door.

April came over to our table and reached for our plates, but Brayden stopped her. "I'll take care of these and lock up. Why don't you go?"

"Okay, I'll leave you two alone then." She flashed me a quick smile, then she traded in her apron for her coat from behind the counter and exited through the kitchen door.

After she was gone, Brayden picked up our plates and took them to the kitchen, and I figured I would sit and wait for him.

Then I noticed that Marissa had accidentally left a glass on one of the tables, and I decided to help and bring it to the kitchen. When I got in there, Brayden was on his phone.

"Next Tuesday sounds good. I'll tell my sister you're the health inspector, so she doesn't ask me why you're looking around and taking notes."

I set the glass down in the sink, and he looked up, his eyes brightening as he saw me there.

"Okay, thanks, I'll see you next week," he said, then hung up. After typing something into his phone, he set it down and came over to me.

"I'm so glad you're here, Sunny. I missed you yesterday," he said, pulling me in for a long hug.

"I missed you too, Brayden." I relaxed, snug in his warm embrace. When he let me go, I stepped back and reached up to play with the collar on his shirt as I said, "You look really nice today. And I'm glad I got to see you in your suit earlier. You looked even more handsome than usual."

"Thanks, you look beautiful today, too," he complimented me. "I guess we were reading each other's minds when we were picking out our clothes this morning, weren't we?" The two of us looked down at our sweaters, and both laughed.

"I guess so," I said, looking back at his face.

"But I think we've been reading each other's minds a lot these past few days." He stepped closer to me, moving like a man with a purpose. "I think you know how bad I've been wanting to kiss you. Ever since I saw you standing under the tent Saturday morning, I've wanted to, and it's all I can think about."

"Me too, Brayden. I was hoping you would have kissed me that first night," I confessed, my eyes not leaving his.

"I know. I saw it in your face. And it wasn't just as we were saying good night, either. I saw the way you were looking at me after I hugged you at the snowman competition. I knew I could have kissed you then." An affectionate smile took over his face as he lifted a hand and caressed my cheek. "But that wasn't the right moment for us."

With one last step, there was no space left between us—his body pressed against mine. I reached up, and my fingers grazed his strong, chiseled jaw, his clean-shaven skin feeling so smooth. With him now this close to me, I picked up his scent—a slight trace of aftershave, having faded throughout the day.

Yet again, his face lingered right in front of mine, not rushing any part of our intimate moment. Unlike last time though, my heart wasn't pounding. It was slow and calm, just like his breathing. The way he was touching me and looking at me made me feel so safe and cared for, and I was happy we waited. Now was the right moment for us. His affectionate smile was the last thing I saw before my eyes slowly closed.

His lips gently brushed against mine, and I knew—in that first instant—that this was the kiss I had waited for my entire life. I could feel the emotion radiating off of him—emotions I have never felt before in a man's kiss. He wrapped his arms around my back and pulled me in closer, his hands gently stroking my hair—and I knew this wasn't just any kiss for him. His feelings intensified the longer he kissed me, and I never wanted him to let me go. I tightened my arms around him and leaned in even further, hoping he knew how I felt. He kissed me for what felt like a blissful eternity until he gently moved his hands to cup my face and rested his forehead against mine.

"Sunny," he whispered. There was so much emotion in his voice as he said my name. "I need you to come with me. There's somewhere I have to bring you."

He pulled his face back, and I opened my eyes and met his. The emotion in his eyes matched that of his voice, and I couldn't quite put a name to it. He picked up my hands and held them to his lips as he closed his eyes again. His breath was heavy against my hands, and after a long moment of silence, he opened his eyes and said, "Please say you'll come with me. I promise you can trust me."

"I know, Brayden," I said quietly. And I really did know it. The look in his eyes and the way he just kissed me told me how much I meant to him.

"So you'll come with me?"

I nodded.

His face softened into a relieved smile, and he gave my hands one last, long kiss before he said, "I just need to lock up, and then we can go."

We grabbed our coats, and as we headed for the door, I couldn't help but wonder where he was taking me. All I knew was that I felt safe with him, and the kiss we just shared confirmed all of my feelings over the past few days.

Chapter 12

♥

WE WERE NOW STANDING in front of a white, two-story Cape Cod-style house with black shutters. The classic look was offset by an orange front door, giving it a vibrant pop of color. A long porch with bird feeders hanging from the roof spanned the entire front of the house. To the left of the front door sat a table with four chairs, and to the right were two rocking chairs, all made from matching cedar. They looked so beautiful, and I knew meticulous care went into making them. Off to the right of the house was a two-car garage attached through a breezeway.

"This is where I grew up. That was my room up there," Brayden said, pointing to the upstairs window on the left. "My mom still lives here." Looking around, he said, "I don't see her car, though; she must be at April's." He was quiet for a second, then added, "And that's good. I was hoping we would be alone."

I turned to look at him, and he stepped toward me, slowly closing the gap between us. He reached forward and gently pulled my hands out of my coat pockets, and as soon as he felt them, he said, "Sunny, your hands are freezing!"

I looked back at his car, the only one parked in the long driveway, and said, "I left my mittens in your car."

He had let go of my hands, and when my attention returned to him, I watched as he unbuttoned the top of his coat. He picked my hands back up and tucked them under his scarf, holding them tight against his chest.

"Is that better?" His smile was as soft and warm as his sweater.

I nodded and whispered, "Thank you, Brayden."

"Thank you for coming with me, Sunny," he said quietly. "But my mom's house isn't why I brought you here. There's somewhere else we still need to go. Somewhere I could never bring anybody." He tightened his grip on my hands, and I could feel his heart pounding through his sweater. The emotion in his voice after kissing me returned, which I could now clearly identify. It was vulnerability. And that vulnerability was in his eyes as he said, "Until I met you." He closed his eyes and leaned his forehead down against mine, his breath heavy against my face.

I didn't say anything; I just stroked his hands with my thumbs. I could feel the vulnerability radiating off of him, and whatever the reason, I wanted him to know that I was here for him.

After a long moment, he straightened up and took my hands out of his coat. Still holding tightly onto one of my hands, he led me around the side of the garage. Some distance out in the backyard, in front of a perimeter of pine trees, sat a large, red, two-story barn. There was a single path shoveled through the snow leading out to it, and his grip on my hand tightened the closer we got. He stopped a few feet in front of the door and stood there for a few seconds, staring at it.

I could feel a thickness in the air, and I knew there was some deep significance to him bringing me here. He let go of my hand, silently stepped forward, and pulled the large, heavy wooden door aside. He returned to stand before me, taking my hands once again. But this time, it felt different. His tight grip from a moment ago was replaced with a much gentler, more relaxed touch. I looked from our hands up into his face, which was now softer, with a peaceful look in his eyes. It was as if opening the door was symbolic somehow, and he was now ready to let me in. He turned, so we were both facing the barn, and slowly led me through the door.

Brayden flipped on the light, and I looked around. It was a woodworking shop. Pegboards lined the walls with numerous tools hung up on them. Tables and benches with large saws and drills sat throughout the room, and several toolboxes were stacked on top of one another. Various projects, including clocks, tables, and picture frames, all in varying stages of completion, were set up throughout the room. It smelled like fresh wood shavings, like someone had recently been working here. I noticed everything was well organized, and all the tools were clean. Even the floor looked like it was swept regularly. Whomever this space belonged to; I felt they took excellent care of it and everything inside.

"This is my dad's workshop," he said, taking our coats and setting them on one of the benches. "We spent a lot of time in here together when I was growing up." He had a far-off look in his eyes, like a flood of childhood memories were coming back to him by being in here.

"I've been wondering about your dad. I've met the rest of your family, but not him."

He didn't say anything, his silence telling me everything I needed to know.

I turned to face him, tears welling in my eyes. "Brayden, I'm so sorry," I whispered. "What happened?"

"He died a few years ago in a car accident," he replied quietly, his voice getting emotional.

I picked up both of his hands in mine. I wanted him to know that I was here to support him, and I patiently waited for him to be able to speak.

After a minute, he let out a deep, steadying breath. "This was my dad's favorite place. We would come in here and spend hours working on projects. He taught me everything he knew about woodworking. I still come in here all the time; it helps me feel closer to him." He looked around with fondness in his eyes like he could sense his dad's presence.

"I still remember getting the call from my mom, telling me he died," he continued. "I almost didn't pick up my phone. My desk was covered in so much paperwork that

I thought I would never get caught up. But she didn't usually call me in the middle of the day, knowing how busy I always was. I figured it might be something important, though, so I mindlessly answered it. I didn't hear her voice right away, so I almost hung up, thinking she had called me by mistake. Then I heard Sam's voice. He had taken the phone from my mom because she was too distraught to speak. He told me my dad had been in a head-on collision, and by the time the paramedics got to him, he was already gone. The doctors told my mom he probably died on impact." He stopped and brushed the back of his hand across his eyes. "At least he didn't suffer, but we never got the chance to say goodbye."

"Brayden," I said, tears now streaming down my face. "I am so sorry that you and your family had to go through that."

"Thanks, Sunny," he said, sweetly wiping the tears from my cheeks. "The odd thing is, the guy in the other car walked away, practically unharmed. They took him to the hospital to check him over, but other than a couple of bruises, he was fine. My mom and April met him, and he was so apologetic—but the truth is, the accident wasn't his fault. It had been snowing, and they both lost control of their cars. My dad just happened to be the one that pulled the short straw."

"Did you get to meet him?"

"No, by the time I arrived, Mom and April were already home. My drive back to Vermont had been slow, between traffic leaving the city and the weather here. Besides, I didn't really need to meet him, and especially right after it happened, I didn't want to. Don't get me wrong, I was glad he was okay, but it just felt so unfair. Why did my dad have to die, but he got to live? Then, after some time had passed and the dust had settled, I stopped asking why. I stopped trying to connect pieces that didn't belong in the same puzzle, and I came to the conclusion that sometimes bad things just happen to good people. Life actually got a little easier after that, once I had made peace with everything."

I held his hands, listening, knowing how hard this must be for him to talk about.

"After his funeral, I decided to move back home to be closer to my family. I realized that life was too short to be spending twelve hours a day in a windowless office. That's when April and I finally opened the bakery she had always dreamed of. She needed some direction at first with the business plan, but then I just sat back and watched as she mapped everything out, right down to the last detail. It hadn't been that long since our dad died, and it was nice to see her excited about something again. Her face looked so happy as she planned out the menu, the look of the interior and exterior, and even the uniforms. And as you saw, I had no input on that last part," he said with a small laugh. "But I wanted it to be an expression of her since she would be the face of the business. I'm just the guy behind the scenes, making sure all the numbers work out."

"Your sister sees you as more than just the numbers guy Brayden," I said to him. "As soon as I met her, she told me that's how you see yourself—but I know you're so much more to her than that."

He nodded and said, "I know how grateful she is. There are times when it's just the two of us in there together, and she'll quietly thank me. She tells me that sometimes she can feel Dad in the bakery with her, just like how I feel him in here."

He retrieved a framed picture from one of the pegboards, brought it over, and handed it to me. Brayden was dressed in a cap and gown, standing outside with his family, and his parents looked so proud. "That's the day I graduated from Syracuse."

I looked from the picture to Brayden's face, then back down again, focusing on his dad. "You look like him," I said. "You have the same kindness in your eyes."

"Thanks, Sunny," he said, smiling at me. "It makes me feel good that you can see that. My dad was a good and kind man, and I always try to treat people in a way that would make him proud."

I looked at the picture again, and this time something else caught my attention. Brayden had his arm around his sister's shoulders, and both of her arms were wrapped around his waist. They had big smiles on their faces like they had just been laughing about something.

"Did you and April get along well growing up?"

"We did. It was important to my parents that my sister and I grew up as friends. It wasn't too often that we got into a disagreement, but when we did, they always encouraged us to work it out and forgive each other. And she knows that all she has to do is pull out the 'Brady,' and I'm over it," he said with a little laugh. "I love running the bakery with my sister; that's why I always work so hard. I feel like I'm doing work that actually matters now. I'm helping my sister to make her dreams come true. Plus, I know she and my mom love baking together, which is the ultimate bonus."

"Did they always do baking projects together?"

"Yeah, they would be in the kitchen on weekends while we were out here. April would always ask our dad what he wanted her to make, and he would always give her the same answer, 'Something sweet.' Then we would see them hours later and compare our newest creations."

"Did you and your dad make all the furniture I've been seeing everywhere?"

"He mostly made the cedar furniture on my mom's porch, but I would help him whenever I came home to visit. And then April asked me to make the coffee table and end tables in her living room a couple of years ago when they bought their house."

"What about the beautiful counter that's in the bakery? Did you guys make that together?"

"In a way, yes," he said, taking a deep breath and then going silent.

When he spoke again, his voice was quiet. "That counter was the last project my dad worked on before he died. He always believed in April growing up, knowing how talented she was in the kitchen. He said he was going to make her a live edge maple counter, for when she finally opened that bakery she was always going on about." He stopped and smiled for a moment like he was reliving a fond memory of his dad and sister together. "When I came back to Vermont, and my mom told me he had been working on the counter the day before he died, I knew I had to finish it—for him and for April."

He lovingly traced his finger over his dad's face one last time and returned the photo to the pegboard. He came back over and wrapped his arms around me for a long, silent moment, and I sensed newfound ease in his embrace. When he let me go, I looked up into his face and saw a man now free of a heavy burden. He picked up my hands and once again held them against his chest, and I instantly noticed that his heart was no longer pounding. It felt calm and relaxed, like by opening up to me, a huge weight had been lifted off of him, and he could now breathe again.

Now I was the only one still carrying a heavy burden, a weight I needed to get off my shoulders. As I looked into Brayden's eyes, I saw such affection and sensitivity, and I knew I could open up to him and let him in, just like he had done for me. Being in his dad's workshop made me feel very close to him, like he brought me here for a reason. This was the opportunity I had been waiting for. Now it was my turn to be vulnerable. Now it was my heart that was pounding.

"Brayden," I started, then I looked away from him, unable to say anything else as tears filled my eyes.

"Sunny," he said softly. "What's wrong?"

I was still quiet and looking away from him, unsure how to start.

"Whatever it is, you can tell me." He was caressing my hands that were still held against his chest. I looked back at him; his expression was so gentle and kind that I knew I could trust him.

"There's someone I need to tell you about," I said, tightening my grip on his hands.

"It's okay Sunny."

And from the caring tone in his voice, I knew it would be okay. My hands relaxed a little, and my heart slowed as I took a deep breath.

"I was married for a few years," I began. "To someone who didn't treat me very well."

"I'm so sorry, Sunny," he said as he gently brushed the tears from my cheeks.

"I wanted to call off the wedding, knowing I was making a mistake, but I had a lot of conflicting thoughts and emotions. I was hoping that things would get better after we got married, but I was wrong. And the more time went by, the worse things got. He became possessive and controlling and treated me like I was his property. I was never his equal."

I looked away from Brayden as I continued talking. "But the really sad part is that the longer I was with him, the more dependent I became on him. Being with him had stripped away all of my self-worth and self-confidence, and it got harder and harder to do things on my own. The whole time I was with him, I wanted so badly to leave him—but I just couldn't. He always lured me back in, making me think I couldn't survive on my own." I shook my head. "It's unbelievable what being with someone like that will do to you."

Brayden put his hand under my chin and gently tilted my face in his direction. His expression was so compassionate as he said, "It wasn't your fault, Sunny. He was manipulating you."

"I know that now, but at the time, he made me believe that I was nothing. All of his lies and threats seemed so convincing; he was a master at playing mind games. The entire time I was with him, I was walking on eggshells, scared to make him mad. He would blow up at me, and I knew I had to take it. I learned really quickly that standing up to him would only make it worse, so I would say or do anything just to keep him pacified. And I ended up hating him—and myself."

"Why did you hate yourself?"

"Because being with him turned me into a completely different person. I went from being positive and happy to angry and bitter. People still called me 'Sunny,' but it didn't feel right. My sunniness had disappeared, replaced by a dark cloud that lingered over me. It got to the point where I couldn't even look in the mirror anymore, ashamed of who I had turned into. I was so miserable, and I knew I was going to stay like that for as long as I was with him."

"So what gave you the courage to leave him?"

"One fight was all it took. I knew at that moment that I had had enough. I still remember how angry he was; it was the most scared I had ever been. He stood there screaming at me, and as usual, I just sat there and took it. Then, all of a sudden, he was over it, and we went on with our evening, just like nothing had ever happened. I played it off in front of him, but I knew right then and there that I was done taking his abuse. I called my parents from work the next morning in hysterics, and that's when we started planning my escape."

I took a deep breath and ran my hands through my hair, silent for a moment before I could continue. "But even after I decided to leave him, I was still doubting myself. Even though getting my freedom back was what I had wanted for such a long time, I found myself panicking in the lawyer's office. I remember sitting there, as she was drawing up the paperwork, thinking, 'Whoa, is this really happening? Can I really do this?' Once the documents were filed, there would be no backing out. He would know that I had officially left him and was serious this time. And that terrified me. At least by staying, I knew what I was getting myself into, but if I left, I had no clue what was going to happen." Then I added quietly, "Plus, leaving him meant I was going to have to survive on my own. That was the scariest part."

Brayden stayed silent as he listened to me, supportively holding my hands, letting them go only to wipe away the tears that kept falling.

"But I knew there was a better life out there for me, so the next morning when he left for work, I packed up Ellie and a few things and ran. It's funny how little you need to take with you when you leave a situation like that. I left in such a panic that I didn't even stop to grab my shoes," I said, shaking my head. "I drove to my parent's house in my slippers." I took a deep breath, still trying to stop the tears. "Walking out that door is the hardest thing I have ever done," I whispered.

I looked off into the distance for a minute, the fear I felt that day coming back to me. When I looked back at Brayden, his face was full of genuine admiration as he held my hands tighter against him and said, "But you did walk out that door, Sunny. You should be so proud of yourself."

"Thank you, Brayden," I replied gratefully. "And I am really proud of myself. It was so hard at first, but things got easier as time went on. What especially helped was when I permanently cut off all communication with him. That allowed me to regain control of my life, and I started to return to my old, cheerful self. I wasted so much time being angry and bitter when I was with him, and that's not who I really am. Being happy and optimistic is who I really am. Once I was free of all that negativity, the dark cloud that had been following me disappeared, and the real Sunny returned."

"The Sunny that I know," Brayden said, smiling at me.

"The Sunny you know," I confirmed with a smile that mirrored his. "And the more time went on, the better person I became. I realized that I no longer hated him or myself. While I was with him, I knew I could never forgive him if he stayed in my life. But once I was completely done with him, I was able to forgive him, as well as myself. And that forgiveness set me free."

"So you forgave him?"

I nodded.

"That's incredible Sunny. Not everyone would be able to do that."

"It was really for me. All the negativity I felt towards him was only hurting me, not him. I knew I had to forgive both of us to be happy and move on with my life."

He was quiet for a moment like he was pondering something. "The thing I don't understand is that you said you forgave yourself too. What did you have to forgive yourself for?"

"For marrying him when I knew I shouldn't have and for letting him treat me like that for as long as I did." I was quiet for a second, then I continued, "And also for the person I had turned into while I was with him. I know I wasn't pleasant to be around during that time. Self-reflection can be hard, and honestly admitting who I had turned into when I was with him wasn't easy. But once I let it all go, I was truly free."

Brayden looked at me with the most compassionate expression as he said, "I am so sorry you had to go through that, Sunny. No one should ever be treated like that, especially someone as sweet as you. And then to forgive him and take so much responsibility for something out of your control is incredible. And to still be smiling is even more incredible."

"Thank you, Brayden," I said, looking at him with heartfelt gratitude. "It's up to each one of us how we handle what life throws at us, and I would rather look on the bright side since that's what the real Sunny does. The real Sunny is always the positive one in the room, finding the good in every moment, no matter what." I reached up and touched his face as I said, "And the real Sunny is a hopeless romantic. And I promised myself that I wouldn't let my experience with him leave me closed off to finding love. True love. I remained optimistic that there was a genuinely great man out there for me, and I just had to wait for our paths to cross." I stroked his cheeks as I added, "And the part of me that I'm the most grateful to have gotten back is my self-confidence. That self-confidence is what allowed me to go to the bakery by myself on Saturday morning and then come back to see you again on Monday. The person I had turned into for a few years would never have been able to do that."

He smiled gently at me and said, "Thank goodness for self-confidence."

"Thank goodness for self-confidence," I agreed, my smile mirroring his.

And just like that, I was now free of my burden.

Brayden took my hands in his, looked me in the eyes, and said, "Sunny Jackson, you truly are one of a kind. Given how positive and happy you are, I would never have guessed that you had been through all of that. My family is right, something has been happening to Mr. Serious these past few days, and it's all because of you. It feels so right having you in here with me."

"Thank you, Brayden, for bringing me here; I can see that your dad's workshop means a lot to you. And I feel like being in here, I've gotten to know him." I stepped closer to him as I said, "And I feel like we've gotten to know each other better here too. Thank you for sharing everything with me and making me feel safe enough to share my story. My past life isn't easy to talk about, but something about being in here made me feel like it was okay to open up to you."

He ran his fingers through my hair as he said, "Thank you for coming with me, Sunny; I'm glad you feel so safe with me. I know it can be hard to open up about the difficult moments in life, but it feels great that we did. And you're right. My dad's workshop really does mean a lot to me. That's why you're the only person I've ever brought here. I've known for a long time that there was only one person I would ever be able to share this place with." He cupped my face in his hands as he said, "And I knew it was you, Sunny, as soon as I kissed you." Then, he leaned in and kissed me with the same soft smile from when we were at the bakery.

I was enjoying another blissfully long kiss, melting further into him as he wrapped his arms tightly around me when the door opened.

"Hey Brayden, don't freak out. I just need to borrow a—" The voice suddenly stopped.

We both turned toward the door to see Sam standing there, wide-eyed.

"You need to borrow a what, Sam?" Brayden asked as he put his arm around my shoulders and kissed me on the side of my head.

He still didn't say anything. He just slowly looked back and forth between the two of us.

"Sam?" Brayden raised his eyebrows at him.

"I need to borrow a hammer, the one with the red handle," Sam finally replied, but he seemed very distracted.

Brayden pointed to a large tool chest along the wall and said, "Top drawer."

Sam kept his eyes on us as he made his way over to the tool chest, taking his attention off us just long enough to look for the hammer. As he was rummaging through the drawer, another voice came—this time starting from outside, growing louder as it got closer.

"Sam, hurry up! If my brother realizes you're in here, he'll have a—" April stopped as soon as she stepped inside the workshop. She just stood there, staring at us like a deer in the headlights.

"I'll have a what April?" Brayden asked his sister, with an amused tone to his voice.

"Nothing," she replied blankly.

April stood paralyzed in her spot as Brayden stepped behind me and leaned down to rest his chin on my shoulder, sliding his arms around my waist. Once Sam had found what he was looking for, he returned to stand in front of us, and April stepped forward to join him. All of their movements were in slow motion, like they were in some alternate universe, unsure what to make of their surroundings, their eyes fixed on us the entire time.

As soon as she was next to her husband, April felt around for his free hand. Holding onto it with both of hers, she said, "Look, Sam, Sunny's here with Brayden."

"I know," he replied.

"In Dad's workshop."

"I know," he repeated.

"Okay, so you see her too?"

He slowly nodded, but she wasn't looking at him. They just stood there and stared at us, no one saying a word. I wasn't quite sure what was happening right now, so I turned to look at Brayden for an answer. I moved slightly to get a better view of him, but his face gave up nothing. He seemed very calm, his peaceful smile a stark contrast to their stunned expressions. He gave me a gentle kiss, then wrapped his arms tighter around my waist.

The silence was broken by Lauren's approaching voice, an urgency in her tone. "What is wrong with you two? You've been out here way too long, and you know how Brayden feels about people being in your father's workshop."

She came in the door and immediately stopped, just like Sam and April had. But unlike those two, she didn't stay that way for long. After a couple of seconds, overcome with emotion, she stepped forward and pulled me into a tear-filled hug.

"Oh, Sunny," was all she could manage through her sobs.

Now it was my turn to move in slow motion. I picked up my arms and delicately wrapped them around Lauren, and as I did so, she tightened her grip on me, her sobs becoming stronger. I wasn't sure what to do, so I affectionately stroked her back. I heard a noise from a few yards away, and I gradually lifted my head to see tears running down April's face. I still wasn't sure what was going on, but my empathetic side took over, and all three of us ladies were now crying. I tightened my arms around Lauren, and as I stood in her embrace, I felt an enormous significance hanging in the air. Just like I had earlier, standing outside with Brayden right before he opened the door to come in here.

After a long moment, I felt Brayden's hand gently squeeze one of Lauren's, and she pulled back to look at me. She lovingly smiled at me as she softly wiped away the tears from my eyes. Then she cupped my face in her hands and quietly said, "You are a very special girl Sunny, and I am so happy that Brayden brought you to Alex's workshop. I was so afraid I would never see this day, but here you are." Then she shifted her focus to her son, her eyes filled with a mixture of love and relief.

Turning around to face April and Sam, she said, "Come on, you two, let's give your brother some privacy." She put her arm around her daughter, and the three of them walked out the door together, closing it behind them.

"What was that all about?" I asked Brayden once we were alone.

"Just my family needing to work on their poker faces," he replied like he was trying to downplay their reactions to seeing me here.

Then he pulled me in and wrapped me in a tight hug, burying his face in my hair. I slid my arms around his waist and lifted the bottom of his sweater, tucking my hands inside. It felt so warm and cozy between his shirt and sweater, and my arms relaxed like they were being supported in a little hammock. I felt a comforting familiarity in his embrace like I had known him my entire life. And as I stood in his arms, I knew he felt it too. There was something in the way he was holding me that made me feel like I was the most important person in the world to him. Like he had been waiting for our paths to cross as well. It just took thirty-two years and a last-minute change of plans to make it happen.

As I was processing everything that had happened here, I snuggled in even deeper, knowing that this was exactly where I was meant to be. I was still confused by his family's reaction to my presence in his dad's workshop, but I knew that when the time was right, all would be revealed to me. In the meantime, I just wanted to enjoy the present moment.

Chapter 13

♥

IT WAS NOW SATURDAY morning, and I was at work. I hadn't seen Brayden's family since they discovered us in his dad's workshop. The spa had been very busy all week with the out-of-towners taking advantage of the freshly fallen snow, perfect for skiing, so I was lucky to have gotten a couple of days off earlier in the week. I was between appointments when I checked my phone and noticed a new text message:

Hi Sunny, it's April. I hope you don't mind Brayden giving me your number.

Hi April, of course, I don't mind. How are you?

It was nice to hear from her, as I always enjoy visiting with her at the bakery. Luckily, she replied immediately since my next massage starts in a few minutes.

A SUNNY DAY IN WINTER

I'm good, thanks. Can you stop by the
bakery later? It would be nice to catch up.

Brayden and I have plans for the evening anyways, so
there's no reason I can't stop by and chat with her first. It
made me feel outstanding that she wanted to see me.

Sure! My last appointment was canceled, so
my hands will get a slight break today (yay!!),
and I'll be leaving work an hour early.
I'll come by when I'm done here.

Great! See you soon!

I smiled as I tucked my phone into the cabinet in my
room and went out to greet my next guest.

A couple of hours later, with four happy guests behind
me for the day, I quickly tidied my room and headed out
the door. I was in Chester before I knew it, walking into
the bakery to be greeted by Marissa's smiling face behind
the counter.

"Hi, Sunny," she said cheerfully.

"Hi, Marissa," I replied, as my attention was pulled to
the loud voices I heard coming from the other side of the
kitchen door.

The bickering got louder as the door opened and April
said, "I told you to stay out of my kitchen!" I laughed as I
watched her push her brother out with an annoyed look

on her face. Her expression immediately changed when she saw me.

"Sunny!" She had a massive smile as she came up and hugged me.

"Hi, April." That was all I could say because she was still talking.

"Your boyfriend here"—she jerked her thumb in her brother's direction—"is making a mess in my kitchen. I'm about ready to toss him out of here."

"Hi, Sunny," he said, giving me a hug and a kiss. "I didn't think you were coming until later."

"I invited her," April snapped at him, still clearly annoyed. "I am allowed to be friends with my brother's girlfriend, aren't I?"

I just watched the two of them with amusement. I love how they get along so well one minute; then they're bickering the next.

"Of course, you're allowed to be friends with my girlfriend," he replied, but he stayed looking at me while he said it. "And I'm happy my sister is being nice to one of us, at least." He pulled his eyes from me to look at April.

"I'm nice to her because she doesn't annoy me. Unlike somebody." She looked at her brother with her arms crossed and her eyebrows raised in irritation. They stared at each other for a moment; then, her face softened into a resigned smile as she added, "And because she makes you happy."

And just like that, I knew they were back to being friends again.

A SUNNY DAY IN WINTER

"You look cute today, Sunny," Brayden complimented me.

"Thanks, Brayden," I beamed at him. "I haven't changed yet; I came straight from work."

"You can change if you want to, but I especially like the yoga pants." He smiled with admiration as his eyes scanned my outfit. "Plus, I'm dressed in my typical week-end attire." He was wearing track pants and a navy-blue hoodie over a white t-shirt.

"And he wondered why I told him to shave and dress nicely last Saturday," April said to me, rolling her eyes. "So, what can I bring you for lunch, Sunny?"

"I'll have a 'Cassidy' and a coffee, thanks," I replied. "The grilled cheese here always tastes so much better than when I make it at home, but that's probably because I always burn mine."

"I don't know about you two," she said, shaking her head and laughing good-naturedly. She turned to her brother and said, "I'll be right back with your lunch as well; you're still not allowed in my kitchen." She swatted him with her towel and then headed for the kitchen door.

Brayden took my hand and led me to our table by the fireplace, and as we sat down, I said playfully, "So I'm your girlfriend now, huh?"

His eyes were sparkling as he looked at me. "We all know not to argue with my sister."

"I learned that a week ago," I said with a laugh. "But that's okay. It worked out really well for me."

He smiled at me and reached for my hands, intertwining our fingers. "So now that I'm officially your boyfriend, when do I get to meet your family?"

My eyes lit up at hearing his words. I know it's a big deal for a man to meet a woman's family, and it made me feel honored that he's the one who brought it up. Although I guess it does make sense, considering I met his family before I even met him.

"I'll call my parents and set something up," I said, my smile mirroring his. "I know they're excited to meet you. I told my mom about you before we got together on Wednesday."

April showed up at our table and heard the tail end of our conversation.

"You should have your parents meet Brayden here. This way, Mom and I can meet them too, and they can see our family business," she said, her eyes bright with excitement.

"They would love that," I said to her. "Especially my dad. As soon as he discovered I met a man who owns a bakery, he's been calling me every day, bugging me to bring him here." I looked at Brayden and said, "I know he wants to meet you, but the person he really wants to talk to is Sam. He wants to find out what it takes to be an official taste tester."

They both laughed, and April said, "I think we can figure something out for him. But right now, our lunches are ready. I have a table set up for us over there, Sunny." She pointed to a table in the front corner of the bakery.

Brayden started to walk with us when his sister stopped him. "Not you, just us girls. I put your lunch over there." She pointed in the opposite direction of where we were headed.

He raised his eyebrows at her.

"Sunny's mine right now"—she tucked her elbow inside mine—"you can have her when we're done." They stared at each other for a few seconds before she added, "Besides, you won't be eating alone."

Just as she said that the kitchen door opened, and Kyle and Cassidy came running into the room. Cassidy grabbed his hand and said, "Uncle Brayden, come have lunch with us."

Kyle was holding coloring books and a box of crayons and added, "And Mom said we can color at the table, but we have to be careful."

Between the expectant looks on the kids' faces and April's serious tone, Brayden knew he wasn't winning this one. He smiled at me and said, "Have fun with my sister. I'll see you in a little bit." Then they headed over to the table set up for them, Cassidy chatting all the way.

April and I went over to our table, and as soon as we sat down, she was looking at me with a smile that was eager for details. "So, what exactly happened after I left you two alone here the other day?"

I laughed and said, "As his sister, I don't think you want all the details, but I will tell you that we finally got the moment we were waiting for." A huge smile spread across my face as I added, "And it was perfect."

"I'm so happy for you two, Sunny," she said, her eyes brightening as she reached across the table and took my hand. After a moment, her expression changed to confusion as she asked, "So, how did you end up in my dad's workshop?"

"After your brother kissed me in the kitchen, he told me he needed to bring me somewhere. I wasn't sure where we were going, but I have to admit, I didn't think it was going to be a woodworking shop."

"He didn't tell you where he was taking you?"

I shook my head. "But there was something in his eyes and in his voice that told me I could trust him. And that I needed to go with him."

"How much did he tell you about our dad?"

"He told me about his accident." I squeezed her hand sympathetically. "I'm so sorry, April."

"Thanks, Sunny," she said with an appreciative smile. "Did he tell you how much my dad's shop means to him?"

"He did. He said no one else goes in there. And I got the impression when Sam walked in on us that he was afraid Brayden might get upset with him."

"Yeah, he prefers to be alone while he's in Dad's shop. What else did he tell you?"

"He told me that the two of them would work on projects together while you and your mom were in the kitchen baking. And he told me about the counter," I said, looking up front. "I noticed it as soon as I walked in the door a week ago. It's so beautiful, and it must be nice having a project they both worked on here."

"It is." She looked at the counter and smiled. "That counter means a lot to all of us. It's like there's a little bit of Dad in here with us." Then she turned back to look at me again. "Brayden has done a lot for the bakery, and not just the counter. He knew how much my dad wanted to see my dream of owning a bakery come true and how much he believed in me. That's why he approached me about going into business together. I had the kitchen experience, and he had the business know-how. He said it was the perfect combination."

"So, it was Brayden's idea to open the bakery?"

"It was. He even put up all the money to get us started and keep it going until we became profitable. I couldn't believe my brother was willing to give up a huge Wall Street promotion just to come back home and open a bakery with his little sister," she said, shaking her head.

"A Wall Street promotion? He told me he worked twelve hours a day in a windowless office," I said, hardly believing what I was hearing.

"Yeah, he was in a windowless office, but then they told him about this huge promotion they wanted to give him. Some new fancy title, I don't remember now what it was, but it was going to come with a corner office and a big expense account. He was going to be managing a lot of important clients, or something like that. You know I don't really listen to him. It sounded boring to me, but he was so excited about it."

"So, what made him change his mind?"

"My dad died," she said simply. "He said he had a long drive back from the city, long enough to think about what was really important in life. He thought the fancy job title with the corner office was what he wanted, but as he was driving home to his new reality, one that no longer included our dad, he felt his priorities change. We saw a completely different person in him as soon as he showed up in my mom's kitchen that night. He even stepped in and basically planned our dad's entire funeral by himself. Brayden's always been good about standing back and letting people figure things out for themselves, but he also knows when he's really needed. My mom was in no shape to make a lot of the decisions, and he knew it, so he took over to lighten the load for her. She gave some input, but it was amazing to watch him stay so calm and make decisions based on what he thought our dad would want. Like I told you a week ago, my brother is not a very emotional man. The only time I have ever seen him cry was during the funeral. It was like once our dad had been put to rest, then he allowed himself to grieve. And it was later on that day when he told me we needed to open the bakery."

"And that's when he moved back to Chester?"

She nodded. "Sam and I went with him to the city to help him pack up his things, while Mom stayed here and looked after Kyle and Cassidy. Mom asked him if that's what he really wanted, or if he was just making an emotional decision in the face of a recent tragedy. He told her that he knew Dad would want us all to be happy and still live our lives to the fullest, even though he was no longer around. He said he realized that his life in the city was not what was going to make him genuinely happy—not even close. He said coming back to Vermont and helping me make my dream come true would bring him the fulfillment he was missing from his life." She paused for a moment, the appreciation written all over her face. "Pretty amazing, huh? There are days I still can't believe he did all that for me."

"I knew right from the moment I met him that he's one of the good guys, but wow, April, you have quite the brother."

"Brayden is definitely one of the good guys; my parents made sure of that," she confirmed with pride in her voice. "And if you think he's a good brother, I guarantee you he will be an even better boyfriend. My dad was an easygoing man, but the one thing he was strict about was that the two of us always needed to be polite. He was especially strict with Brayden regarding how to treat a woman, always reminding him to treat a lady with kindness and respect."

"It's good to know there are some parents still raising their sons to have respect for women." I was quiet for a second, looking down at our table. Then I looked at April and said, "Did Brayden tell you I was married? It's okay if he did."

She nodded and said, "I'm so sorry you had to go through that, Sunny. I know Brayden would never treat you like that."

"Thanks, April. It was a tough time in my life, but I learned a lot. And after living with someone like that, it makes me appreciate a great guy even more." I looked at the table where Brayden was sitting with the kids. They had finished their lunch, and the three of them were coloring and laughing, with Cassidy in her usual spot on his lap. I watched them for a moment before I turned my attention back to April.

"And I know your brother is different. There is something so special about him. He's like no one I've ever met before. And it's more than just his personality." I paused for a second, the emotions from the other day returning to me just as strong now as they were then. "You keep saying that he's not a very emotional man, but there was some serious emotion radiating off your brother a few days ago. What I felt while he was kissing me in the kitchen and then again standing in your mom's driveway before he took me back to the barn was like nothing I've ever experienced. And then actually being in your dad's workshop with him?" I paused again, shaking my head, still curious about the significance of the place.

"I don't know, April...But there was something about being in there with him the other day; it's like he brought me there for a reason. A big reason. And it wasn't just because of your reactions when you saw us. I could feel it before he even opened the door."

Her eyes were sparkling as she gently smiled at me and said, "All I can tell you is that my dad's workshop means the world to Brayden, and for him to share it with you is a bigger deal than you know. I promise you, Sunny; my brother sees something in you that he has never seen in anyone else."

Our lunch was now finished, so we stood up, and she gathered our plates and cups.

"Thanks for having lunch with me, Sunny; I'm glad you were able to stop by. I'll let you go now and be with Brayden. I really am happy for the two of you."

"Thanks, April," I said with a smile. "And thanks for texting me and inviting me to lunch. I had a good time." She gave me one last smile, then turned and headed into the kitchen.

I stood there and watched Brayden with the kids for another minute, still thinking about everything April had told me. He must have felt my eyes on him because he looked over at me, his eyes brightening as he realized I was alone. He slid Cassidy off his lap and came over, pulling me into a warm embrace. I felt even more at home in his arms this time, my affection for him deepening as I learned more about him.

"I'm all yours now. Miss Bossy Pants said so herself," I declared with a playful smile as he let me go.

"Good," he said, the brightness in his smile matching his eyes. "There's somewhere else I want to bring you."

Chapter 14

♥

WE WERE NOW BACK in Lauren's driveway, and once again, Brayden's car was the only one there. He took my hand and led me around the garage, and as we got closer to his dad's workshop, we took a different path in the snow—this one bringing us to the back of the building. I followed him up a set of stairs leading to a large deck with lights wrapped around the railing, giving it a festive and welcoming feel. A cedar table sat off to one side, similar to the one on Lauren's porch. The only difference was that it was smaller and had two chairs instead of four. Open land surrounded both sides of the deck, and we were pretty close to the line of pine trees, making for a lovely, private setting. It was so peaceful and quiet, the kind of place you could spend hours enjoying a good book in the fresh air. Or the company of a wonderful man.

Brayden smiled as he saw me admiring the view, and he came up behind me and wrapped his arms around my shoulders.

"It's so beautiful up here," I sighed peacefully, resting my hands on his forearms and leaning back against him.

"Yeah, I love living here," he said, breathing in the fresh air.

"This is where you live?" My smile perked up even more as I turned to look at him, his excitement to share this place with me glowing in his eyes.

"My dad and I renovated the top of his workshop during the summers when I was home from college. It used to be all open space, but we turned it into an apartment. Come on; I'll show you what we did."

An incredible feeling came over me as soon as I stepped through his door, something I had never experienced walking into a space for the first time. I felt instantly at home in his apartment, like I could spend the rest of my life here with him. Some kind of force kept pulling me in further, telling me that I belonged here, and I knew there was nowhere else I wanted to be. I stopped halfway into his living room, looking around wide-eyed, admiring his home and all its welcoming glory.

"Brayden, this place is unbelievable," I marveled, turning to look at him.

"Thanks, Sunny," he accepted my compliment with a proud smile.

His living room and kitchen were open concept, with beautiful knotty pine walls in the living room leading up to a high, sloped ceiling. Live edge maple counters wrapped around the perimeter of his kitchen, sitting on top of cherry cabinets constructed with masterful detail.

The pale, calming green color of his kitchen walls contrasted nicely with the natural wood everywhere else. Two large windows brightened his kitchen—one overlooking his deck and the other facing the expansive land next to the building. Gorgeous wood grain and quirky knots gave personality to the yellow birch flooring, and even though there were many different types of wood throughout his place, they all complimented each other. In the corner of the living room was a wood stove with a glass door—the perfect balance of warmth and ambiance.

Regarding furniture, he had a matching ivory loveseat and chair, an oak end table, and a small dining table with two chairs made from maple. Several maple frames adorned the walls, some with photos of family in them, others of beautiful scenery. It was a relatively small apartment, making it so cozy and welcoming. That, and the man who occupies it.

"You and your dad did all of this?" I admired out loud, my eyes still huge with awe as they landed on him.

"And the best part is that we had fun doing it." His eyes were sparkling as they met mine. He set our coats on the back of the loveseat, and then he took my hand, excited to show me more. "We decided to make two bedrooms, and I'm glad we did. I use this one as my office."

My attention was immediately caught by a long desk made of maple and walnut arranged in a herringbone pattern. "Brayden," I gasped, touching the desk and looking at him. "Did you make this?"

He nodded. "Since I often work from home, I knew I needed something bigger than my little dining room table." He smiled as he looked at his desk. "This was my first attempt at herringbone."

"It's beautiful," I breathed, delighting in his creativity.

"Thanks, I'll show you what else I made." His eyes shone with pride as he led me into the more oversized bedroom. The room's focal point was a mission-style headboard and footboard with rectangular spindles framing a queen-sized bed, a nightstand on one side, and a dresser sitting along the opposite wall—all constructed of curly maple. The furniture design was perfectly understated, letting each board's unique personality be the true star of every piece. "I made all of this once I moved back to Vermont after I finished the bakery's counter."

"Your woodworking is such a gift Brayden." I slid my arms around him, leaning my head against his shoulder. "It makes your home feel even more warm and personal."

"Thanks, Sunny," he beamed, tightening his arms around me. "When I'm not working on stuff for the bakery, I'm downstairs having fun with a project. My mom and April think I don't take time off, but they don't realize how much time I spend in my dad's workshop. They think that just because I don't sit down that I'm not relaxing, but woodworking is my release when I need to take a break from the bakery."

"So, what did you do to relax while living in New York?" I asked him.

He thought for a second, then said, "I really didn't relax when I lived in the city. I would go out with friends occasionally, but that didn't happen all that often. My life in New York revolved around my work, with long days spent in the office and then going home and working some more."

"April told me during lunch today that your company had offered you a promotion, but you turned it down to come back to Vermont. She said it was your idea to open the bakery."

He unwrapped his arms from me and led me back into the living room. We sat down on the loveseat facing each other, and he took my hands in his.

"Yes, it's true that the investment firm I worked for had offered me a big promotion. And yes, I turned it down. At first, I didn't, though. When they approached me with this new opportunity, I was so excited. I was finally going to get out of the cramped, windowless office I shared with another guy. He was so jealous when I showed him the office they were going to give me, but I knew deep down he was happy for me. He was just going to miss me. And I was going to miss him too. We spent three years in that tiny shoebox together, and we hit it off right from day one." He stopped talking for a second, pausing to reminisce about his old friend.

"But then, when I found out that my dad had died, all of my priorities changed in an instant. The fancy job title and private office I had worked so hard to achieve no longer meant anything to me. I felt like there had to be more to life; I just wasn't sure what it was yet. Plus, I had other things to focus on at that moment, like planning my dad's funeral."

"Your sister told me you pretty much planned it all yourself."

"I knew my mom was having a tough time when she couldn't even decide on the flowers, so I jumped in to try and make things at least a little bit easier for her. She had just lost her husband of thirty-two years; she didn't need to be worrying about details that weren't important. She did make some decisions, though, like to keep his wedding ring versus burying it with him. Those are the things that really matter when the love of your life dies unexpectedly."

I silently listened as he spoke, rubbing my thumbs on the backs of his hands. A warm adoration spread through my heart at hearing his deep insight and dedication to his family.

"After the funeral, several friends and family members were gathered in my mom's kitchen, eating and reminiscing about my dad. And while I liked hearing old stories I had forgotten about, I needed to remember him in a different way, so I grabbed my coat and went out to his workshop. It was my first time being in there since he died; I couldn't bring myself to go in before that. I felt his presence as soon as I walked through the door, and I started having a conversation with him. He always encouraged me to figure things out for myself, but I told him I desperately needed his help this time. I was stuck, feeling

159

like I needed a new direction in my life—a real purpose. That's when I noticed a new picture on his workbench, one I hadn't seen before. I went over and picked it up, and all of a sudden, I felt peaceful. It was the first time I felt relaxed in days, and I knew at that moment that my dad was showing me the answer I had been looking for. So, I went back into the house and told my sister I wanted to open the bakery with her."

"What did she say?"

"She turned me down," he answered matter-of-factly, shaking his head.

"Why did she do that? You were offering to help make her dreams come true."

"She was scared. She had a job, and although it wasn't her dream, it was something safe and familiar. If she left, she would be venturing into uncharted territory, and that terrified her."

"I can relate to that," I said sympathetically, remembering my previous life.

"I repeatedly tried to assure her that she has what it takes to own a business and that I would be with her every step of the way. I even told her I would put up all the money so she wouldn't have to worry about the financial aspect. But that really backfired on me because then she got scared that she was going to lose all my savings. After a week of struggling to convince her, I knew I had to pull out my one trick that always works on her. Just like her calling me 'Brady' gets my attention, there's only one thing I have to say to get hers. Whenever I tell her, 'I believe in you, April;

you need to believe in yourself,' I always see an instant change in her. I don't know if it's because she realizes at that moment that I truly do believe in her or if she just wants to shut me up—but it works every time. She was finally ready to sit down and start a business plan for the bakery she had dreamed about her whole life."

"She must have been excited to make her vision a reality, getting it all out on paper after dreaming about it for so long," I said to him, my eyes brightening. as I imagined April planning out her beautiful bakery.

"Eventually, yes. But she got frustrated at first, not knowing where to start. So, I told her just to write out how she would describe it to our dad. He always listened so patiently to her; she constantly jabbered on about it the whole time we were kids." He laughed like he was reliving a memory of the two of them. "So that's what she did. I gave her some help with it, guiding her through the important details to think about, but everything you see at the bakery is what she had always envisioned since she was a kid. And I was so proud of how she took charge and made it her own. Just like how she took charge when she and Sam were helping me pack up my things to leave New York."

"She told me they helped you."

"Did she tell you what she did with my furniture?"

"No, she left that part out," I replied, and by the grin on his face, I figured this was going to be a good story.

"My family hadn't ever been to my apartment since they weren't into 'visiting the big city,' as they put it, so

I always came back here to see them. As soon as April walked through my door, she immediately informed me that none of my furniture was coming home with us. I asked her what was wrong with my furniture, and she said it looked like it belonged in a college dorm room. When I told her that I did, in fact, get my futon and beaten-up chair in college, she put her hands on her hips and said to me with a commanding voice, 'Brayden Alexander Montgomery, you are thirty years old. It's about time you get some grown-up furniture.' Then I made the mistake of telling her that she sounded like our mom."

"You said that to your sister?" I asked, my eyes huge with amazement.

"Yup. I did," he confirmed, pressing his lips together.

"Brayden, as a fellow female, I can tell you that's one of the worst things anyone can say to us." I was laughing as I said it, surprised that he was unaware of this fact.

"Oh, I found that out for myself about twenty minutes later," he said, laughing as well. "As soon as I said it, April stormed out of my apartment, and Sam and I just looked at each other and shrugged. We each grabbed some boxes, and he got started in the kitchen as I went into my bedroom. I was sorting through my closet when he peeked his head in and told me I needed to come into the living room. I got out there just in time to see two men carrying my futon out the door, and when I asked what they were doing, April told me they were from the Salvation Army, and she was donating all of my furniture."

"She did that to you?" I said, still laughing.

"Yeah, she gave them everything too—my futon, my beaten-up chair, even my bed. I still remember the look on her face as she brought them into my bedroom and made them wait while she yanked off my sheets, wadded them up, and crammed them into the garbage, ranting about how they probably hadn't been washed in a year. The only thing she let me keep was this oak end table," he said, gesturing behind him. "My dad and I made it while I was in high school, so she told them they couldn't have it, but everything else went. I just stood there and watched as most of my stuff either went out the door with two strangers or into the trash. When Kyle gets older, I will definitely warn him never to tell a woman that she sounds like her mother. That's one lesson a man should never have to learn the hard way."

After we both stopped laughing, I said, "Brayden, I am so sorry, but that really is funny."

"It's okay; I agree with you. It was thoroughly entertaining to watch my sister like that. And now I can get away with telling her she sounds like our mom; it's become a running joke between the two of us. And truthfully, she was doing me a favor. My furniture was quite hideous and in desperate need of an update." He leaned in close, his eyes sparkling as he said, "I'll let you in on a little secret about us guys. We really don't care what our furniture looks like; we just care that we have something to sit on." We shared another laugh, then he continued, "Besides, with my furniture out of the way, there was a lot less to pack, and we didn't have to worry about getting everything into two vehicles. The back of Sam's truck was practically empty, thanks to Miss Bossy Pants and her little rampage. But then, on the way home, I knew something was wrong when Sam pulled over before we even left the city."

"Why? What happened?" I questioned. He was looking down at our hands, fidgeting with my fingers. When he looked back up at me, his expression had turned serious.

"I was following the two of them, and I figured we would stop at least once along the way, but we were only on the road for about ten minutes before April made him pull over at a gas station. In the middle of rush hour traffic, no less. So I pulled over as well, and as soon as I got out of my car, my sister came up to me crying. She wrapped her arms around me, sobbing, and I looked at Sam for an answer. He told me that she felt horrible and needed to talk to me right now—and in person. I tried to understand her, but I learned years ago that it's impossible for my sister to cry and talk coherently at the same time. I barely understood a word she said, but what I did manage to catch was, 'I'm really sorry, Brady.' And as usual, I instantly felt bad. I knew I should have told her in my apartment that I didn't care about my stuff, and I think it was just now sinking in what she had done. So I told her it was okay, and she even rode home with me. It was during that ride when I told her that standing in my apartment, watching her give away all my stuff, I knew—with absolute certainty—that she has what it takes to own a business. Even though my sister can be quite bossy with other people, she can sometimes struggle with her confidence—especially when it comes to something life-changing. Business ownership is not for the faint of heart, and I saw the confidence in her that I knew existed all along; she was just too afraid to let it out. That's when I told her I really believed in her and that she needed to believe in herself. Then she was ready to start working on a business plan."

"So you still hadn't convinced her to open the bakery before you packed up all your things?"

"No, it wasn't until we were driving home from New York that she finally agreed, but I knew deep down that she would eventually be on board. I was just waiting for the right time to remind her that she could do it. I needed the perfect way to convince her that she has what it takes—and the way she took charge like that in my apartment was the opportunity I had been waiting for. So I let her know. I gave her the confirmation that she needed."

"I think it's really sweet the way you have so much faith in your sister. To turn down a big promotion and pack up your life before she even agreed—not every brother would do that," I said, amazed at his unwavering belief in her.

"Thanks, Sunny," he said, smiling at me. "And I put my faith in her again when I gave her my credit card and told her to go and pick out some new furniture for me."

"April picked out all of this?" I asked him, looking around.

He nodded. "It was my way of making it up to her for telling her that she sounded like Mom in my apartment.

165

Plus, I liked the ideas she was coming up with for the bakery and knew she would do a good job around here too. When she asked me what I wanted, I told her to surprise me because, again, I'm a guy, and I really didn't care. The only stipulation I gave her was no pink," he said, with a little laugh.

"She did an excellent job," I complimented her design choices.

"I think so, too. It feels a lot more like home than my apartment in New York ever did. Besides, her taking care of things around here gave me time to start working on the financial side of opening the bakery. Initially, I tried to get April involved with the money aspect, teaching her about costs and margins, but I noticed her thoughts always seemed to be elsewhere. I knew she was imagining the look and feel of the bakery—the stuff she was excited about. So I let her off the hook with the business side of everything, figuring it would be easier if I took care of it myself. We would always agree on the big picture, then I would go back to my computer, and she would go back to menu and decor planning. And as you can see, it's three years later, and she still doesn't want to be that involved in the financial side of things."

"I got that impression the other day when we were waiting for your meeting to get done," I said with a little laugh, remembering April's impersonation of her brother. "She said she can only take so much of hearing about your five-year plan."

"Ah yes, my five-year plan," Brayden said, laughing as well. "What my sister doesn't realize is that my five-year plan is actually coming along better than expected—and I'm working on a surprise for her. I'm lucky she can't read my writing since there were details on that notepad she was looking at the other day that I didn't want her to see."

"Does your surprise have anything to do with the health inspector phone call I overheard when I went into the kitchen?"

He nodded. "Fortunately, my sister has always put a lot of trust in me, and she doesn't ask too many questions. We've worked exceptionally hard to make the bakery a success, and I can't wait to see the look on her face when everything comes together." He ran his fingers through my hair and said, "And the bakery means even more to me now that I have a girlfriend to share my success with. Everything feels different since I met you, Sunny—especially my favorite spot in the bakery. It feels much more intimate now."

"It's my favorite spot, too, Brayden. I love how cozy and romantic it is. And I only sit there when we're together—it wouldn't feel right to sit there without you."

"That's because April set it up for couples," he said, smiling at me. "As she started arranging everything, she noticed how private and out of the way our table sat from all the others. The fireplace was already there; the previous tenants put it in. She said it seemed so romantic—like a little haven where happy couples could sit and enjoy each other's company, without having anyone else around."

"And I noticed the flowers on that table are different too."

"She does that to make it feel even more special and unique. She's always changing the type of flowers on our table—it seems like they're different every time I look over there. April even came up with the idea for one coat hook. She said that couples could hang up their coats together, and it would look like they were hugging." He was quiet for a second, then said, "And I'm happy that I get to share that coat hook with you, Sunny."

"I feel the same way, Brayden," I agreed as I moved closer to him—a wave of happiness flooding me. "And your sister's right. I noticed it the first time you hung up our coats and scarves together—they really did look like they were hugging. And it feels amazing to hear you call it 'our spot' and 'our table' because I think of it as ours too."

"Sunny, everywhere I look now, I see as our spot—as somewhere for us to share," he said as he slowly ran his fingers down the length of my hair. "The table in the bakery, my dad's workshop—and now my home. All of these places were special to me before I met you, but I always knew something was missing. And now there isn't anymore."

"Thank you, Brayden, for wanting to share all of your special places with me," I replied, my feelings of belonging intensifying. "Especially your home. I have such a strong feeling that I belong here. I felt it as soon as I walked through your door."

A SUNNY DAY IN WINTER

He cupped my face in his hands and smiled softly at me. "That's because you do belong here, Sunny."

And then, with that soft smile still on his face, he leaned in the last few inches and kissed me. He wrapped his arms around me and pulled me into him, the intimacy between us deepening. I snuggled in even closer, knowing that in his arms was where I felt truly at home.

Chapter 15

♥

IT WAS NOW THE following Saturday, and I just showed up at the bakery after work. I traded my yoga pants for a dress before leaving the spa since my parents are meeting us here soon. We decided to get together on the weekend, so my parents could meet everyone, including Sam and the kids. I've been having a great time getting to know Brayden and his family, and I'm excited for all of them to meet my mom and dad. As Brayden came through the kitchen door, April was finishing with a customer at the counter.

"Just the man I was looking for"—the gentleman handed an envelope to Brayden—"here you go. Usually, I mail these, but I couldn't resist stopping in again."

"Thanks," Brayden said, sliding the envelope into his laptop case.

The man returned his attention to April. "Your bakery is quite impressive. My wife is still raving about the treats I brought home for her last time. I'm sure she'll love these just as much." Then he picked up his bag and headed out the door.

Brayden came out from behind the counter and hugged me. "Hi, Sunny, you look extra pretty today."

"Thanks, Brayden, you look very handsome yourself. I like this sweater on you; it's my favorite one so far." The collar of a white shirt with a windowpane pattern was folded neatly over a crew neck navy-blue sweater that he had paired with khakis, and his face was clean-shaven.

"Thanks, I want to make a good first impression. Meeting the parents is a big deal."

April came up to us, and after greeting me with a hug, she turned to her brother. "That guy was the health inspector, right?"

"Yup," he answered casually.

"Why was he inspecting the outside of the building the other day? They don't usually do that."

He shrugged. "I guess the state of Vermont must have some new regulations."

"Aren't you going to look at his report?" she asked him, fidgeting with her rings.

He nodded. "I will later—but I know there's nothing to be worried about."

"Who's worried?"

"You are," he replied matter-of-factly.

"I am not!" she retorted. The high pitch of her voice suggested otherwise.

He raised his eyebrows at her—clearly not buying it. They stared at each other for a few seconds, then he

171

looked down at her hands and said, "You fidget with your rings whenever you're nervous about something."

She opened her mouth to say something, but he stopped her.

"You have ever since you were nine—when you got that gaudy yellow ring out of a gumball machine." His expression softened as he gently pulled his sister's hands apart and said, "Everything is fine, April. And I don't mean fine like how you say it when you're mad at Sam or me."

She sighed and rolled her eyes, looking down at her hands that were still in his.

"Look at me, April." She shifted her eyes back up to his face. "Have I ever steered you wrong?"

She shook her head.

"And what did I tell you when we opened the bakery?"

"To believe in myself and to trust you," she said quietly.

"And you have this entire time, right?"

She nodded.

"So don't start doubting us now, okay?"

"Okay," she agreed. I could see her anxiety fading as she looked at her brother—secure in their partnership.

"And remember, we have two very special guests on their way to see this amazing business we built together." He let go of his sister's hands and slid his arm around my shoulders.

April's expression instantly changed—her face brightening as she looked at me and said, "We're all so excited to meet your parents, Sunny. Thanks for agreeing to bring them here. I'll go check on Mom and see if she needs any help putting the final touches on everything." She turned toward the kitchen, stopped, and faced her brother with a grateful appearance. "Thanks, Brayden," she said quietly, hugging him. "You've always been the one person who knows what to say to make me feel better."

"You're welcome, April," he said as he hugged her tighter. "That's what I'm here for."

Once she was gone, I looked at Brayden and said, "Wow! She really does put a lot of trust in you."

"Yeah, she always has." He ran his fingers through his hair, a flash of guilt passing over his face. "I feel kind of bad not being straight with her, but I'll come clean on everything when I surprise her next month." Then he stepped closer to me, his voice lowering as a mischievous grin took over his features. "And it's a big surprise too. Mr. Executive will even be making an appearance."

"Well, I would love to see that," I requested, smiling at him as I played with his collar. "Mr. Executive is very sexy in his tailored suit."

"I would love to have you here, Sunny," he obliged as his face inched closer toward mine. "Even though the surprise is for my sister, I especially want to celebrate with my girlfriend." Just as he was about to kiss me, the kitchen door opened, and April, Lauren, and the kids entered the room.

"Sunny!" Cassidy ran up and hugged me.

"Hey, pretty girl," I greeted her with a smile. I noticed her brother standing behind her, being his typical, quiet self. "Hi, Kyle."

"Hi," he said with a shy smile.

Lauren hugged me and said, "We're so happy your parents are coming here to meet all of us, Sunny."

"Me too," I concurred, looking at everyone's excited faces. "They should be here soon."

As if on cue, the door opened, and in walked my parents, their smiles growing as I went over to hug them. I took their coats and draped them over a nearby chair, amused as I watched the two of them for a moment. My mom wore a burgundy flannel shirt with black corduroy pants—my dad's favorite thing to see her in. Her short, salt and pepper hair was clipped back in a purple barrette, her brown eyes sparkling as she looked around. My dad was in his typical attire, a long-sleeved casual shirt unbuttoned enough to reveal the top of his t-shirt—this one with donuts printed all over it, and khaki pants. His buzz-cut gray hair was shimmering under the lights, and his hazel eyes were as huge as a kid in a candy store.

I led them over to everyone and started the introductions. "This is Brayden, his mom Lauren, his sister April, and her kids, Kyle and Cassidy. These are my parents, Rob and Natalie."

The ladies exchanged pleasantries with my folks, then Brayden shook my parent's hands and said, "It's nice to meet you, Mr. and Mrs. Jackson."

"It's nice to meet you too, Brayden," my mom said with a warm smile. "And please, call us Rob and Natalie. We're not big on formalities."

A SUNNY DAY IN WINTER

The gleam in my dad's smile matched that of his eyes as he looked around and said, "This place is even better than Sunny described it." Then his focus landed back on Brayden's family, and after scanning them one more time, he looked at me expectantly.

I grinned at April. "You know who he's waiting for."

"Samuel!" she called out over her shoulder.

The kitchen door opened, and Sam walked in carrying a tray. "Sorry I wasn't out here already, but I was putting together some samples for my new taste testing partner." He set his tray on the table next to us and extended his hand to my dad. "Sam Fournier."

"Rob Jackson," my dad said, shaking his hand. His eyes brightened up even more as they landed on the assortment of treats. "Those look great. Donuts are my favorite food group."

"Mine too!" Sam exclaimed, eagerly pulling out their chairs. "Cool shirt," he said as they sat across from each other. "You'll have to tell me where you got it."

And just like that, my dad had a new best friend.

"Let's leave these guys to their goodies," April said with a laugh. "We can order lunch for them."

The rest of us stepped up to the counter as Marissa came out of the kitchen.

"Wow, Sunny!" she said, her eyes huge as she saw us. "You look just like your mom."

My mom and I looked at each other, and both laughed. "Yeah, we get that a lot. Marissa, this is my mom Natalie, and that's my dad Rob," I said, gesturing to the guys enjoying their little party.

They exchanged pleasantries, then she looked over at the excited taste testers, her pretty blue eyes dancing with amusement as she watched them together. "It looks like Sam's finally met his match." She shifted her focus back to us and said, "So what would everyone like for lunch?"

We placed our orders, and Lauren went into the kitchen to help Marissa while the rest of us rearranged a couple of tables to accommodate our large gathering. The kids were also helping us—Cassidy chatting my mom's ear off the entire time and Kyle not saying a word.

"I will agree with you, Sunny." My mom smiled as she watched them together. "These two are just like you and Russ."

"Right?" I said with a laugh. "I had them figured out as soon as I met them."

Brayden glanced over at my dad and Sam enjoying their donuts and smiled at me as he slid his arm around my shoulders. "I see what you mean about having your dad's outgoing personality. They've only known each other for a few minutes, but they look like they've been friends for years."

"Yeah, all of the friendly genes definitely came to me!" I said as I watched them.

Lauren and Marissa returned from the kitchen a few minutes later and set out all the food and drinks. As everyone took a seat, April called to the pair bonding over their donuts, "Come on, guys."

My dad sat next to my mom and looked at the sandwich she had ordered for him, his eyes brightening even more. "Donuts and peanut butter and jelly? This place keeps getting better and better."

"Everyone here has a sandwich named after them," I explained to my dad. "You have 'The Brayden.'"

"A man after my own heart." My dad looked between Brayden and Sam, giving them both a thumbs up. "You two are top-notch."

I couldn't help but smile at my dad. He is so easy to please. Give him donuts and peanut butter and jelly, and you'll have a friend for life.

"So Natalie, did Sunny have a favorite sandwich growing up?" Lauren asked my mom.

"Yeah, she and Russ loved fluffernutters; I made those all the time for them when they were kids. Sunny always had to have hers cut on a diagonal." My mom smiled at me.

"I didn't know Marshmallow Fluff was a New England thing until I left home for the military. The rest of the country doesn't know what they're missing out on," I said, shaking my head and smiling.

"Did you bake with your kids while they were growing up?" My mom asked Lauren.

"April and I did, but I banished Brayden from the kitchen after he made a batch of cinnamon rolls that were so salty, we couldn't even eat them."

"Maybe I should have done that," my mom said with a laugh. "I would bake with my kids when they were little, and Sunny would make a big mess every time. She couldn't even stir neatly. I would always tell her, 'Keep it in the bowl, Sunny,' but she always got ingredients all over the counter."

"Don't worry, Natalie, we've already banished her from our kitchen," April said, grinning at me. "As soon as we found out about her bread."

"The one from home ec class?" My mom asked me, her expression turning from a smile to a look of exasperation.

I nodded.

"You told them about that?"

"About an hour after I met her." Brayden smiled at me.

"I still don't know how she did that," my mom wondered aloud, shaking her head.

"I do." My dad briefly took a break from his sandwich to join the conversation. "Sunny inherited my mother's cooking skills. That's why she always burns her grilled cheese. I grew up on burned food, so it's no big deal to us—is it Sunny?"

"No," I said with a laugh. "It has to be totally charred for us to throw it away."

"Yeah, we heard about the grilled cheese, too," April added, still smiling at me.

My mom just sighed.

"Well, on the bright side," my dad came to my defense, "at least you met a man who's okay with eating peanut butter and jelly. Even you can't screw that up, Sunny."

Brayden kissed my hand and said, "It's okay. Sunny's sweet personality makes up for her lack of cooking skills."

The two of us shared a smile, and I noticed out of the corner of my eye that my parents were doing the same thing across the table. I know they're happy I've found a great man who accepts me exactly as I am—horrible cooking skills and all.

AFTER EATING, WE CONTINUED to sit and visit, and both families enjoyed getting to know each other. Cassidy had climbed onto Brayden's lap as soon as she finished her sandwich, leaving her chair free for Marissa to join us after her shift was over. Everyone here has been so lovely to me since the moment I met them, and I felt even more accepted as they all took an interest in my parents. It was now late afternoon, and my folks decided to get going.

"Sam"—my dad shook his new friend's hand—"it's been a pleasure."

"Same here, Rob," Sam replied jovially. "I'll let you know about any new creations to try."

My dad gave Sam an acknowledging smile and thanked the ladies one last time. Then he turned his attention to my boyfriend and put his arm around Brayden's shoulders. He led him away from the group, but I could still hear them as they spoke.

"Brayden, you are a true gentleman, and I can see that you make my daughter happy—and that makes me happy. Welcome to the family."

"Thanks, Rob," Brayden replied, shaking his hand. "Your daughter is very special to me, and I will always treat her right." Pure happiness spread through me as I watched—my boyfriend's face alight as he told my dad how much I meant to him.

My mom hugged the ladies goodbye and said, "Thank you so much for your hospitality today. Rob and I feel very welcome here. Sunny told us how friendly all of you are, and she said you made her birthday unforgettable. I'm overjoyed that she found all of you, especially Brayden." She looked at him for a second, then turned back to Lauren. "Thank you, from one mother to another, for raising a gentleman. My daughter deserves an exceptional man, and I'm so happy they found each other."

"Thanks, Natalie," Lauren said, taking my mom's hands in hers. "My husband and I are very proud of Brayden." Then she looked at me and smiled. "And we all feel the same way about Sunny. She really lives up to her name. She's brightened all of our lives and makes my son genuinely happy—which is what every mother wants. And we're delighted that you feel at home here. You and Rob are very much a part of our family."

"Next time, you'll have to bring Russ with you," April chimed in. "We would love to meet him."

"You basically have him right here." My mom smiled at Kyle, who was quietly standing next to April. "But I'll let him know. I'm sure he would love to come by and try your wonderful food. He could be your silent taste tester."

"The more, the merrier," Sam enthused, patting my dad on the shoulder as he and Brayden now stood with the group.

"Bye, Mr. and Mrs. Jackson," Cassidy said, hugging my parents for what seemed like the hundredth time since they got here.

"Bye, Cassidy." The smile on my mom's face gave me the impression that she was remembering me as a little girl. Then she looked at the shy little boy holding his mom's hand and said, "Bye, Kyle, it was nice meeting you."

"Bye," he said quietly, practically hiding behind April.

After the three of us put our coats on, I said, "I'll be right back. I'm going to walk my parents to their car." Brayden and I shared a quick smile, and then I went out the door.

"So, you guys like him?" I asked my parents as we stepped out into the fresh air.

"Sunny, he's wonderful!" my mom raved, tucking her arm in mine as we walked.

"Yeah, Brayden's a real stand-up guy. He gets my vote," my dad agreed.

"Thanks, I figured you would like him." I could feel my smile glowing brighter.

"And his family is amazing; they're our kind of people," my mom said as we reached their car.

"We're so excited for you, Sunny. All we wanted was for you to meet a great man." A gigantic smile spread across my dad's face as he added, "And the fact that he owns a bakery is the ultimate bonus."

We laughed as I gave them each one last hug, then I watched as they drove away. I turned to head back to the bakery, eager to get out of the cold and back into the warm arms of my sweet boyfriend. Plus, something had caught my eye while we were having lunch, and I wanted to get a closer look.

No one noticed when I returned; everybody was busy picking up dirty dishes and rearranging the tables and chairs. That's okay, though; it allowed me to admire one of the pictures on the wall quietly. Even though I've been in the bakery many times over the past few weeks, it just dawned on me that I haven't looked at the photos decorating the space. And since it was hung up behind Brayden, my eyes were drawn to the beautiful maple frame encasing it every time I looked at him.

I set my coat down on Brayden's chair and stepped close to the picture, tears blurring my vision as I realized what I was looking at. It was April and her dad. She seemed to be about fourteen or so, her dad had his arm around her shoulders, and they both had proud smiles on their faces. In her hands, April was holding up a drawing of a red brick building with pink and white striped awnings above the windows and a sign over the door that read *Something Sweet Bakery* in whimsical blue lettering. I was wiping the tears from my eyes when I felt a comforting arm slide around my shoulders.

"That's the picture that inspired me to open the bakery." Brayden had a warm smile on his face as he stood next to me, admiring the photo.

"Brayden, this place looks just like her drawing," I said, my eyes full of amazement.

"Yeah, she had it all planned out ever since she was a teenager—right down to the name," he said, reaching up and touching the photo. "When she was initially setting up the interior, the only input I requested was that this picture be on display. This one image captured her life's dream and how proud our dad was of her. As soon as I saw it sitting on his workbench, I knew my dad was telling me that this was just as much my destiny as it was April's—and I knew what I needed to do."

Brayden turned to look at me and held my hands against his chest as he continued, "But at the time, I just saw it as my professional destiny. It wasn't until I met you that I realized he was also guiding me toward my personal destiny. It's because of our bakery that you came to town. You had to come and try the cake that got such great reviews. It was like my dad knew that this bakery would fulfill both of his kids' dreams and bring each of us what would truly make us happy."

Tears filled my eyes again as I said, "Brayden, I came here by myself a few weeks ago, planning to enjoy my birthday cake quietly, but I got the surprise of a lifetime when you walked under the tent that morning. And by the time we got back here for the celebration you set up for me, I felt like all of my dreams had come true. I didn't even make a wish when you gave me my cake. I didn't need to."

He gently brushed away the tears and cupped my face in his hands, his eyes so full of affection as he looked at me. The soft smile that I love so much was on his handsome face as he leaned in and kissed me, wrapping his arms around me and pulling me in tighter. As I stood in his embrace, my fondness for the bakery grew deeper, knowing that it made all of my dreams come true as well.

Chapter 16

♥

MONDAYS ARE OFFICIALLY MY favorite day of the week. I love waking up to a fresh start on a Monday morning, excited for the seven new opportunities ahead of me. And with the recent addition of pizza and a movie at April's, I now have the perfect foundation for starting the week off on a positive note. I was just about to leave work and head to Chester when my day suddenly felt like a Monday that everyone else could relate to.

"Sunny, can I see you for a minute?" my boss called out as I walked past her office.

"Sure, what's up?" I asked her as I went up to her desk.

"Have a seat." She gestured to the chair against the wall, and I sat down. "One of our guests, Mrs. Harris, complained about the massage you gave her this morning."

My heart sank. I know I'm not in trouble; this happens occasionally. But I always try my best to please my guests, and when someone leaves unhappy, I feel like I've let them down.

"What did she say?"

"That you got oil in her hair, and the pressure wasn't deep enough."

I thought for a second. "I checked with her about the pressure as we got started, and she said it was fine. She mentioned during the intake not to massage her head and to be careful with her hair—which I thought I did. I'm really sorry, Greta."

"It's okay Sunny," she replied, her voice full of understanding. "These things happen sometimes, and I just needed to let you know." I think she sensed my disappointment and wanted to cheer me up, so she smiled at me and added, "But I do have some good news for you."

"Really?" I asked, perking up.

"Warren's mom called today. They're coming to visit next week, and I made sure to book him with you."

My eyes brightened up at hearing her news. "Thanks, Greta!"

"You're welcome, Sunny. Have a good rest of your day. Try not to let this complaint bother you."

I left her office and headed toward Chester. By the time I got to town, the bakery was closed, so I went straight to April's house. I tried to forget about Mrs. Harris's complaint, but it always bothers me when I cannot do my best for someone. I walked into April's kitchen to be greeted by my favorite open arms.

"There's my beautiful girlfriend," Brayden said sweetly as he wrapped his arms around me.

A SUNNY DAY IN WINTER

Ahh, that's better, I thought, letting out a contented sigh and snuggling further into his embrace. When he let me go, I looked up at him and smiled, grateful to have warm arms that comforted me after a disappointing day at work.

Once the pizza was finished, we gathered in the living room, and as everyone was taking their seats, Lauren turned to me and said, "Is everything okay, Sunny? You were a little quiet during dinner."

"Yeah, I'm okay," I sighed. "I just had a bit of a rough day at work. One of my guests complained about the massage I gave her."

"Who would complain about you, Sunny?" April asked me with a confused look on her face.

"Thanks, April." I couldn't help but smile at her.

"Seriously, Sunny—what happened?" Brayden asked me, taking my hands in his.

"She said I got oil in her hair, and my pressure wasn't deep enough."

"People complain about stuff like that?" Sam asked me.

I nodded. "Yup. They do. And the funny thing is, I'll go months without a single complaint, and then it seems like two or three guests will complain about me in the same week. Thankfully I never get in trouble. It's just disappointing, that's all."

Brayden tossed the large turquoise pillow on the floor and said, "Have a seat. You deserve a massage of your own tonight."

My eyes lit up as I looked at my sweet boyfriend. "Thanks, Brayden!" I gave him a kiss, then sat down and leaned back against his legs. "You're so good to me."

"That's what I'm here for." He kissed the top of my head as he started on my shoulders.

"It was Cassidy's turn to select the movie tonight, and she picked Finding Nemo. How does that sound to everyone?" Lauren asked as we all settled in for the evening.

"It sounds great to me," I said, smiling at the little girl sitting next to her parents. I picked up one of Brayden's hands and kissed it, thankful for the magic he was working on my tight shoulders. "I'm feeling better already."

"Wake up, sleepy-head," a deep voice whispered in my ear. "The movie's over."

I opened my eyes to see everyone smiling at me.

"You two make quite the pair," April said, looking at us affectionately. "You had my brother so relaxed at your first movie night Sunny, that we thought he was sleeping. And then you guys switched places tonight, and you actually did fall asleep."

I thought about it for a second, realizing I didn't make it that far into the movie before dozing off.

"That's how you know it's a great massage," I said as I stretched and let out a yawn.

"So, I'm not too bad for an amateur?" Brayden asked, leaning down and wrapping his arms around my shoulders.

I turned and gave him a kiss. "I wouldn't call you an amateur." I smiled at him as I slid my hands over his arms. "I feel so much better now."

"Well, that means I'm doing my job as a good boyfriend." He gave me another kiss; then, he rested his chin on my shoulder as I relaxed my head against his.

"How long have you been doing massage therapy, Sunny?" Lauren asked me.

"Five years." I was quiet for a second, then added, "But I've been thinking about switching careers lately."

"Don't let that lady bother you," April said encouragingly.

"It's not just her. When I first started massage therapy, I loved it—but I've been losing my excitement lately. And now it feels like I'm still doing it just because it's familiar." I paused for a second, sighing. "When I started my life over after my divorce, my job was the one thing that stayed constant—and that was incredibly comforting at the time." I intertwined my fingers with Brayden's and turned to smile at him. "But now I'm in a stable and caring relationship. Where I once looked to my job for safety and comfort—I now have that in you." He returned my smile, wrapping his arms tighter around me.

"So, what are you thinking about doing instead?" Lauren asked me.

"I'm not sure." I felt my smile get bigger as I remembered Greta's good news. "But on the bright side, my favorite guest is coming to the spa next week, and working on him will re-energize me in the meantime."

"That's what we love about you, Sunny," April said with a kind smile. "You always look on the bright side, even after you've had a tough day."

"So why is he your favorite guest?" Brayden asked me.

"He's a young guy in a wheelchair who comes with his mom and aunts once a year to visit from New York. His mom helps to get him into the room and reclines his chair, then she leaves, and he just relaxes peacefully. Sometimes we chat, sometimes he's quiet, but he's always so nice and polite. Whenever I work on him, I remember why I got into the profession in the first place—to help people relax and make them feel better. The nice ones are always the easiest to work on, and they help to make up for the guests that weren't the right match for me."

Everyone was smiling at me as Lauren said, "Well, he sounds delightful, but I can't imagine anyone not being happy to get paired with you."

My focus shifted from their smiling faces to Brayden's handsome profile beside me. He looked like he was contemplating something. He turned and gave me a gentle kiss, then sat back and pulled me up to sit next to him.

"I've been thinking about something lately, too."

April, Sam, and Lauren all switched their attention to him, their smiling faces full of expectation.

"Kyle," Brayden said, looking at his nephew.

"Yeah?" he replied quietly.

"I'm working on a special project in Grandpa's workshop. Would you like to help me with it?"

His entire face lit up. "Really?"

"Brayden," Lauren gasped, putting her hands over her heart. "Are you serious?"

"Yeah, I figured it would be a good way for Kyle to get to know Dad since he was only four when he died. If that's okay with you two," he said, looking at Sam and April.

They looked at each other wide-eyed, then Sam turned to Kyle. "Would you like to help Uncle Brayden?"

He nodded enthusiastically.

April looked at her brother and said, "It's okay with us; just don't let him use any power tools. He's still a little young for that."

"Deal!" Brayden agreed. He studied his family's expressions for a second. "You guys all look so surprised."

"We know how you feel about your father's workshop," Lauren said to him.

"Yeah, and we weren't expecting your announcement to involve Kyle—that's all," April added.

Brayden smiled fondly at his beaming nephew. "It'll be nice to teach the next generation about woodworking. Especially since my favorite memories of Dad are of the two of us in his workshop together."

"And I know he loved every moment he spent in there with you, too," Lauren said, with tears in her eyes. "He would be so proud of you for wanting to share his love

191

of woodworking with Kyle. We're all proud of you, Brayden."

April also had tears in her eyes as she put her arm around her mom and kissed her on the cheek. Then she smiled gratefully at her brother and mouthed, "Thank you."

He silently nodded and smiled at the two of them, watching as they were overcome with emotion at the big step he was taking. Then he turned his attention to me, slid his hands around my waist, and pulled me closer to him. He stroked my lower back as he leaned in close and whispered in my ear, "It'll be nice to have Kyle in my dad's workshop with me, so thank you, Sunny. It's only because of you that I was able to open the door and let anyone else in. My dad's shop has always been very special to me, but it means even more to me ever since you first stepped through that door."

I moved closer to him and wrapped my arms tightly around his shoulders. A warm feeling spread through my heart, knowing that the place he created such fond memories with his dad means even more to him now because of me.

Chapter 17

♥

OLD MAN WINTER WAS loosening his grip on New England, and the first signs of spring were starting to show. The snow had practically all melted, the crocuses were blossoming, and the daffodils were making their way through the soil—promising cheerful pops of color before long.

I was in the bakery on a Wednesday morning enjoying April's coffee break with her when the door opened, and in walked Mr. Executive. My heart swelled as I admired every aspect of his exquisite navy-blue suit accentuating his masculine physique. Underneath his well-fitted jacket was a light-blue shirt, a red and gold striped tie, and gold cufflinks sparkled brightly at his wrists. Every time I see my boyfriend, he grows excessively attractive—no matter what he's wearing. But I must say—there is something about Mr. Executive in his tailored suits that makes him even sexier. I sat back and savored the view, watching his freshly shaven face glowing in the mid-morning sun as he scanned the room. His eyes brightened as they met mine, and his smile grew more prominent with every step as he made his way over to us.

"I have a surprise for you."

"Ooh! Did you hear that, Sunny?" April said teasingly, reaching across the table and grabbing my hand. "Mr. Executive has a surprise for you."

I looked up at Brayden and smiled. "He's not looking at me, April."

Her expression changed as she turned her attention to her business partner, her eyes expanding as she noticed Brayden's smile. He looked at the door and motioned to a group of men standing outside. The door opened, and three men in suits entered, all with smiles mirroring his. He gently took his sister's arm, prompting her to stand—which got Lauren and Marissa's attention, and they came out from behind the counter.

"Do you remember when we first opened this place?"

She stared at him silently—her only movement was when she started fidgeting with her rings.

"It was three years ago today. Happy anniversary, April," he said, his eyes shining brightly.

"Yeah, I know. We have that party planned for tonight," she said, finally able to speak.

"Well, we have more than just our anniversary to celebrate today." He turned to face the men standing on the other side of the table. "Do you remember Mr. Jones and Mr. Cooper, the men I met with from the bank last month?"

She nodded.

"This other man is Mr. Arquette. Gentlemen, this is my sister and business partner, April Fournier."

"It's nice to meet you, Mrs. Fournier," Mr. Arquette said, extending his hand to her.

She just stood there wide-eyed, her fingers still tightly gripping her rings. Brayden gently separated his sister's hands and extended her right hand to the man smiling at her. That broke her from her trance.

"Where are my manners?" she said apologetically. "It's nice to meet you, Mr. Arquette." After she shook hands with the other two men, she turned her attention back to her brother. "What's going on, Brayden?"

"You know my five-year plan? The one that you love so much?" he said with a humorous tone to his voice.

"Yeah."

"What's the number one thing at the top of my list?"

"To buy the building from Mr. Bishop," she answered without hesitation. She turned to the men and said, "I've listened to my brother go on and on about his five-year plan for so long that I know it by heart."

They all chuckled, then Mr. Jones and Mr. Cooper stepped apart to reveal another man standing behind them. He was dressed much more casually, in a blue coat, jeans, and a *Navy Veteran* hat. "Hi, April," he said with a warm smile.

"Mr. Bishop?" April looked at her brother for an answer.

"Mr. Jones is the Vice President of business transactions at the bank, and Mr. Cooper is their attorney. They're here to represent us, and Mr. Arquette is Mr. Bishop's attorney." He picked up his sister's hands. "Congratulations April. What I hoped we could do in five years, we managed to do in three."

Lauren gasped, her hands covering her heart as she smiled proudly at her kids.

"Are you sure we can do this?" April asked her brother.

He raised his eyebrows at her. "Are you seriously questioning my math? Because I have several spreadsheets that I can show you right now."

"Please don't," she said, putting up her hand with a laugh. "I believe you." She paused for a moment, still processing everything. "So how did you make all of this happen without me knowing? We're together most of the time—so you couldn't really do it behind my back."

"Honestly, I did a lot of it right under your nose," he admitted.

"Like what?" She crossed her arms and glared at her brother.

"You know that health inspector who was taking notes about the outside of the building?"

"What about him?"

"He was actually an appraiser. And my notes from my meeting with Mr. Cooper—the ones you were snooping around at?"

"Uh huh?"

196

"Those notes were crucial details about our upcoming transaction." He put his arm around his sister and said to his colleagues, "Fortunately for me, my handwriting is so bad that my sister had no clue what she was looking at."

The men shared another good-natured laugh as Mr. Cooper told April, "My meeting with your brother wasn't even planned that day. But then he and Mr. Jones returned to the bank, and all I heard about was the amazing food here. So I jumped at the chance when Brayden invited me to come and check out the bakery for myself. And I must say, Mrs. Fournier, your cinnamon rolls did not disappoint. This is quite the business you and your brother have built."

Brayden looked at his sister with a massive grin of achievement, and her irritation from him bending the truth instantly vanished.

"You're lucky I like you," she said, playfully swatting at him.

"So, are we ready to make this official?" Mr. Cooper asked.

April smiled at her brother. "Absolutely!"

Lauren came over and hugged her kids. "Your father and I are so proud of you two," she said, with tears of joy in her eyes.

"Thanks, Mom," Brayden said to her, then he led his sister to a large table at the side of the room. Six chairs were already set around the table—enough to accommodate all of them—but I watched as Brayden pulled up an additional seat that stayed empty next to him. He would glance at the extra chair from time to time with a proud smile lighting up his face—like he was sharing a moment with a special guest only he could see.

BRAYDEN AND APRIL WALKED their business colleagues to the door when their meeting was over, as Lauren and Marissa cleared the plates and coffee cups from their table.

"Mr. Montgomery, Mrs. Fournier, it was wonderful doing business with you," Mr. Cooper said as he shook their hands.

"And thank you so much for agreeing to have the closing here instead of the bank," Mr. Jones said, shaking their hands. "It's not every day that I get to oversee a business transaction involving a bakery, and being here was much more pleasant than the bank's conference room. Thank you for your wonderful hospitality."

"I think you just picked up three new happy customers along with a building that's all yours now," Mr. Arquette said. "Congratulations on your success." He shook their hands as well, then all three men exited.

"Brayden, April," Mr. Bishop regarded the proud siblings standing before him. "The two of you have been the best tenants I've ever had. It was a pleasure doing business with you these past three years."

Brayden shook his hand. "Thank you, Mr. Bishop. We couldn't have asked for a better landlord." He put his arm around April's shoulders and said, "You let my sister make this place her own, and I'm very grateful for your flexibility with the changes she wanted to make. Even though you owned the building for our first three years, this place has felt like home to us ever since we first opened our doors. We hope you and your wife will continue to stop in and visit."

He smiled and said, "You will be seeing a lot of Francine and me; you can count on that. Congratulations again." Then he turned and left.

Brayden smiled at his sister and said, "We did it, kid!"

"Thank you, Brayden," she said quietly as she wrapped her arms around him. "For everything. For believing in me. For being patient with me. For never giving up on me." She looked up at her brother. "And I guess even for all the times you wouldn't let me spend any money—and for always forgiving me when I would get mad at you for it. It's because of your tight grip on the finances that we officially own our bakery now." A smile spread across her face as reality sunk in further that she indeed owned the bakery in its entirety now.

"It might be my tight grip on the money that got us here, but your wonderful baking is what kept people coming back." His face glowed triumphantly as he added, "We really do make a great team."

They walked over to Lauren, Marissa, and me, their faces radiating with victory. Lauren pulled her kids in for a family hug, beaming with motherly pride. Marissa hugged the two of them as well—everyone celebrating their big moment. Then Brayden turned his attention to me.

"It feels perfect having you here for this, Sunny," he said, wrapping me in a hug. "I'm so happy you came."

"Thanks for inviting me, Brayden." I smiled at him and reached up to play with his collar. "I always love it when Mr. Executive makes an appearance. And you were right—this is such an exciting surprise for your sister."

"So you knew about this?" she asked me.

"I knew he was planning a surprise for you—but he didn't let me in on any details. Congratulations, April!" I enthusiastically hugged her.

"Thanks, Sunny," she said, tightening her arms around me. "I'm glad you were here for this, too, since you are part of our family." She smiled at me as she let me go, then beamed at her brother again. "I still can't believe you did all of this."

"*We* did all of this," he corrected her, then handed me his phone. "Can you take a picture of us, please, Sunny?"

"I would love to!" I said, excited to capture this momentous occasion.

"Not right now, Brayden," April protested, running her hand down her ponytail. "Let's wait until later—when we're back here for the party. When I'm dressed up, and my hair looks nicer."

He put his hands on her shoulders and shook his head. "No, April. This is who we both are. I'm Mr. Executive in a tailored suit, and you are..." He pushed his sister out to arm's length and scanned her appearance. "Miss Sloppy Haired Baker in a foo-foo apron."

She laughed and swatted him playfully—giving in because she knew he was right. They wrapped their arms around each other and faced me, with tremendous smiles engulfing their features. A warmth of inclusion flooded me as I took their picture, elated that I got to share my boyfriend's big moment with him and his family.

A FEW HOURS LATER, we were back at the bakery for the celebration that April and Lauren had planned a few weeks ago. Marissa was finishing the decorations when we came in, appearing cute in a purple dress and her blonde hair pulled up. April was so beautiful in a dark-blue dress—and I realized this was my first time seeing her dressed up and not covered in flour. Sam, Lauren, and the kids looked cheerful, with Cassidy twirling around in a pink dress and her hair in pigtails. Brayden and I were the last to arrive. We had gone to his place to change our clothes, and he looked handsome in khakis and a black sweater, and I felt elegant in a black dress. He also wanted to put together a gift for his sister—which he discreetly handed to Kyle, who beamed from ear to ear as he excitedly ran to hide it in the kitchen.

"Good, everyone's here now"—Lauren clapped her hands together, smiling at Brayden and me, standing hand-in-hand—"go ahead and get some food. We have a lot to celebrate tonight."

The ladies had outdone themselves. Streamers dangled from the ceiling, and confetti scattered on the tables shimmered happily against the white tablecloths. A beautiful array of tasty treats was set up on several tables, and a *Congratulations* banner hung against the front wall. Candles flickered throughout the room, and the lights were dimmed—setting a romantic and celebratory mood.

Sam took a bite of something new and looked at me with huge eyes that reminded me of someone else. "Sunny, I have got to call your dad and get him back in here. These things are amazing!"

"It would make his day to hear from you, Sam," I said, chuckling. "He keeps asking me how his new best friend is doing and when he's going to see you again."

Brayden led me to our cozy little nook of the bakery, where the fireplace was emitting a warm and welcoming glow. We set our plates down, and he pulled out my chair, then reached for my hands across the table.

"You look so beautiful tonight," he said, his eyes sparkling with affection.

"Thanks, Brayden." I smiled at him as I intertwined our fingers. "You looked so handsome earlier. I like your navy-blue suit as much as the charcoal gray one. And I always love seeing Mr. Executive in action. You look so natural running a business."

"Thanks, Sunny." He smiled quietly at me for a long moment, rubbing his fingers against mine. "It was great having you here while April and I bought the building. This place has meant the world to my sister and me for three years, and it means even more to me now—and not just because we own it. I've been looking forward to today ever since I realized we could make it happen, imagining how excited April would be. But when I looked over at you during our closing and noticed you smiling, that's when I knew I was truly successful. Not only was I going to own a great business with a wonderful partner—but I knew that when I stood up from that table, I would be congratulated by the best girlfriend a man could ask for. Thanks for making this day even more special for me."

"Thank you for including me in your big day Brayden; it was special for me too." I leaned across the table and gave him a kiss. "I know how much this place means to you and your sister, and it means a lot to me too. Your bakery is what brought us together, and I'm so happy I get to be here celebrating with you and your family."

We sat silently, content in each other's company, holding hands across the table while the fire softly flickered next to us. We were pulled out of our private moment by the lights brightening and the sound of April's voice across the room.

"Can everyone please gather around? We ladies have an exciting surprise of our own."

Brayden and I got up and walked hand-in-hand to join his family.

"So, we've been working on something behind the scenes as well," Lauren said, with April and Marissa standing next to her. "We knew we were going to do this tonight, even before Brayden's big surprise earlier."

April was holding a box, and the three ladies stepped forward. "Here, Sunny," she said, handing it to me as their smiles glowed brighter.

I looked at Brayden, and he shrugged and shook his head. "I swear this is a surprise to me too."

I set the box on the table next to me and squealed with excitement when I opened it—my face beaming as I looked at the gift inside. I reached in and pulled out my very own pink and white striped apron, turning to the ladies with a smile that mirrored theirs.

"You mentioned wanting a career change a little while ago," April said. "You're more than welcome to help us here anytime you'd like."

"Really?" I asked, clutching my apron to my chest.

"Really," Lauren confirmed, her eyes glowing as she watched me. "But we're going to put you on the counter, not in the kitchen," she quickly added with a laugh.

"Good thinking. We don't want to scare off the customers with anything I would make," I agreed, laughing as well. After I hugged all three of them, I put on my apron and turned around, beaming at Brayden. "What do you think?"

"I think you look beautiful." He stepped forward and wrapped his arms around me. When he let me go, his smile broadened as he slowly ran his eyes down me and added, "And it only took three years, but now I'm crazy about the foo-foo apron."

A SUNNY DAY IN WINTER

"Uncle Brayden," a typically quiet voice sounded louder than usual. "Can we give Mom her surprise now?"

"Sure, why don't you go get it."

Kyle dashed to the kitchen as April's eyebrows furrowed in confusion. "You have another surprise for me?"

"Yup, we do."

A second later, Kyle was standing next to Brayden with a bag in his hand, with enormous smiles on both of their faces.

"Do you remember that special project I wanted Kyle to help me with in Dad's workshop?"

She nodded.

He gave Kyle a gentle nudge, who stepped forward and handed the bag to his mom.

April shared a smile with Sam and Lauren as she set the bag down and reached in. Her face lit up as she pulled out a maple frame surrounding the picture I had taken of her and Brayden earlier.

"Uncle Brayden let me measure and use sandpaper," Kyle said excitedly.

"And you did a great job!" April praised her son, giving him a hug. Then she looked at her brother with tears in her eyes and whispered, "Thank you, Brayden."

"You're welcome, April." A warm smile spread across his face as he watched his sister—tears rolling down her cheeks as she looked at the picture in her hands. "Do we want to hang it up?"

She smiled at him and nodded, clearly too emotional to speak.

He put his arm around her, led her to another special picture, and said, "We could hang it up next to you and Dad. How does that sound?"

She nodded.

"I figured you would agree, so I snuck in here last night and put up a nail, hoping you wouldn't notice."

She gently batted at her business partner, amazed at his continued craftiness. Then she stepped forward and hung up the photo, her hands lingering on the frame for a moment. Brayden stepped next to her, and she wrapped her arms tightly around her brother, overcome with emotion.

"These two pictures sum up how much Dad and I always believed in you," he said, smiling at his sister. "We're so proud of you, April."

"Thank you, Brayden," she whispered again. Then she reached up, lovingly touched the photo that started it all, and whispered, "Thank you, Dad."

The two of them turned back to face the rest of us—to see that all of us ladies were now crying. They came back to join us, Sam reaching out to hug his wife.

Brayden stepped over to me and gently smiled as he brushed the tears from my cheeks, then he leaned down and wrapped me in a tight embrace. "You are so sweet," I whispered to him. "Everything you do for your sister is incredible."

"Thanks, Sunny," he said quietly. Then he took my hand and led me back to our spot by the fireplace, away from his family. "My dad and I made a pact years ago that we would always support April in her dreams—no matter what. When he died, I knew it all fell on me to make it happen, and I've been working non-stop for three years to make him proud. I know he was with us earlier during the closing; that's why I pulled up an extra chair. I wanted him to have a front-row seat. And I can feel him in here now too. He's standing over there, next to my mom, with a huge smile on his face, so proud of all we've accomplished." He ran his fingers through my hair, a soft smile taking over his handsome features. "And I know he's smiling at the two of us, happy that the bakery is what brought us together. I've thanked my dad every day since I met you for opening my eyes with that picture of him and April. That single picture has made both of our dreams come true on so many levels, and I still can't believe how lucky I am to have you in my life." He clutched my hands to his chest and said, "I love you, Sunny Jackson."

"I love you too, Brayden," I whispered, tears escaping my eyes. "And it feels good to say it out loud finally. I've been telling you inside my head for a long time that I love you. I was just waiting for the right time to say it out loud."

"Me too," he admitted, his smile glowing even brighter as he affectionately brushed the tears of joy from my face. He leaned in and kissed me, pulling me into a loving embrace. This was my favorite kiss so far, and I relaxed in his arms, feeling pure happiness spreading through me at hearing him say aloud what I'd suspected for so long. This was the perfect ending to a day full of sweet surprises—the sweetest one of all saved for last.

Chapter 18

♥

Spring gave way to summer, bringing with it some of my favorite things. Long days full of sunshine and pleasant weather, with the occasional thunderstorm thrown in to heighten the romance of a summer night. In addition to Monday night movies and pizza, mini golf and ice cream became a Friday night ritual. We enjoyed our first Fourth of July celebration, complete with fireworks and a patriotic parade a few towns over.

I've been helping out at the bakery on my days off from the spa, and I love it! I have so much fun interacting with the customers, and my favorite part of all is how cute I feel in my foo-foo apron. Today was one of my days at the spa, and I had just gotten home and sat down to relax with Ellie for a moment—when there was a knock on my door.

"April!" I said excitedly as I opened the door to my unexpected guest.

"Hi, Sunny," she said, coming in and hugging me. She reached down and patted the furry welcoming committee, then stood back up and announced, "I am taking you out tonight for a girl's night."

"Really? That sounds like so much fun!" A huge smile spread across my face. "And you look so pretty; I love this blue dress on you. I just need to shower quickly, and then we can go. Ellie will keep you company in the meantime."

I got ready in record time—stepping out of my bathroom with my makeup on and hair styled thirty minutes later.

"All I need to do is pick out something to wear, and I'll be ready."

I walked into my bedroom to see April sitting on my bed, smiling, holding up a sleeveless black sheath dress. "Why don't you wear this?"

"Sure," I agreed, happy for her suggestion. She helped me with the exposed gold zipper in the back, and I decided to pair the dress with yellow heels, giving the black a vibrant pop of color.

A few minutes later, we were heading out the door. I wasn't sure where we were going, but it really didn't matter. I've liked April ever since I first met her, and it made me feel good that my boyfriend's sister wanted to spend so much time with me. I got the impression that she was also excited to be going out tonight because she kept glancing over at me and smiling as she drove. As we came into Chester, she turned off Main Street onto the road leading to the back of the bakery.

"Marissa texted me while I was at your place. She thinks she left the coffee maker on and asked if I could stop in and check quickly." She pulled into a parking space and smiled at me. "Why don't you come in with me? You can see some new decorations I picked up."

My smile matched hers as I said, "Thanks, April, I would love to."

She unlocked the door, gestured for me to go in first, and then said, "The decorations are out front, behind the counter."

I made my way through the kitchen and realized she was no longer with me as I pushed the door open. Suddenly I was taken back to the night of my birthday—awestruck as I noticed rose petals on the floor. I followed the trail around the counter to see my boyfriend standing in front of our table. He looked irresistible in a light-blue button-down shirt and khaki pants, his clean-shaven face radiant as he silently stepped forward and wrapped me in a tight hug.

"Happy anniversary, Sunny," he said with a sweet smile as he straightened up and looked at me.

"Thank you, Brayden," I replied, my smile mirroring his. "But we already celebrated our anniversary last week."

"That was the anniversary of our first meeting—which I already knew you would want to celebrate. So I planned a second celebration—one to surprise you with." He stepped back and slowly scanned my outfit. "You look magnificent tonight. This is my favorite dress of yours." His eyes were glowing with adoration as they returned to meet mine. "You look pretty in colorful pastels—but you look stunning in black. I was hoping April would pick the right one based on my description."

I shook my head good-naturedly. "You two are quite the pair."

"When I told her I wanted to surprise you, she asked what she could do to help. And she even offered me another pass into the kitchen."

"So, since we've already celebrated the anniversary of our first meeting—what are we celebrating tonight?" I asked, a little confused.

"Six months ago, we officially became boyfriend and girlfriend—which is equally worth celebrating," he said, his eyes glowing brighter.

I laughed as I thought back to that day. "That's right. Miss Bossy Pants was so mad at you when I got here; she was yelling at you for making a mess in her kitchen. She declared us an official couple; then she claimed me for herself and made you have lunch with the kids."

He laughed, too, as he said, "She was on a roll that day." Our laughter calmed as he ran his fingers through my hair, a soft smile taking over his face. "But I definitely wasn't going to argue with her when she called you my girlfriend." He gazed at me fondly for a moment, then took my hand and turned toward our table. "Come on, let's have a seat."

Since there are no windows in our romantic little corner of the bakery, the fairy lights twinkled brighter above us—making it feel even more intimate and magical. Once again, he had set out two plates with sandwiches, two glasses of water, and two cups of coffee. My smile perked up even brighter when I noticed the flowers in the vase between two flickering candles.

"Pink tulips!" I reached across the table and took his hands in mine.

"Of course," he said, his eyes sparkling. "I couldn't forget our official flowers."

We enjoyed our peanut butter with raspberry jam sandwiches while we reminisced about our favorite happenings of the past six months. After we were finished, he got up, grabbed our plates, and headed toward the kitchen. I took this moment by myself to look around and appreciate all the effort this exceptional man goes through for me. My heart swelled with love as my eyes settled on the tulips in the vase—something special to us since day one.

A few minutes later, Brayden appeared from the kitchen with a small, white pastry box in his hands. He set it down in front of me and returned to his seat, his face beaming as he looked at me across the table.

"What's this?" I asked him, my eyes lighting up.

"Open it and see." A sparkle in his voice matched his eyes as he watched me.

I looked from my loving boyfriend down to the gift sitting on the table in front of me. I lifted the lid and gasped, my hands flying to cover my mouth as I beheld the most beautiful sight I had ever seen. Inside the white box was a little cake covered in chocolate frosting, with the words *Will You Marry Me?* delicately written in light pink frosting. I sat there and stared at the cake for a moment, my hands slowly moving down to my heart, surging with love for this man.

"Brayden!" I whispered, tears of joy in my eyes as I looked up at him.

He stood and came to kneel next to me, a bright smile on his handsome face. I pivoted in my seat to face him, and he gently wiped the tears from my eyes, then took my hands in his.

"Sunny Jackson, when I first met you six months and one week ago, I thought you were the most beautiful woman I had ever seen. Right from the first moment I saw you, I knew that there was something very special and unique about you. And then—when the first thing you said to me was that you have a cat named Elephant—that's when I knew there was something really different about you!"

I leaned forward and wrapped my arms around his shoulders, burying my face in his neck as we shared a good laugh. After a moment, I sat back up, our laughter calming, and his kind smile that I love so much returned as he continued, "But it's okay because I knew in that first moment that you weren't afraid to be yourself, and I knew I could be my true self with you and open up to you and let you in. I have let you into places I could never bring anyone else because no one else was worthy of sharing them with. And I'm not just talking about my dad's workshop and my apartment. I'm also talking about my heart. I gave my heart to you as soon as I first kissed you, and it has belonged to you ever since. You have been the best girlfriend a man could ask for—but I don't want you to be my girlfriend anymore."

He reached over to the jacket draped around the back of his chair and pulled a small, black velvet box out of the pocket. My eyes grew huge as he opened it to reveal a gorgeous diamond ring. I looked from the diamond, sparkling under the glow of the fairy lights, up into his eyes that were sparkling just as brightly.

"I want you to be my wife. Sunny Jackson, would you do me the honor of marrying me?"

"Yes," I barely managed to whisper through my tears of joy.

He slipped the ring onto my finger and stood up, pulling me to my feet. He cupped my face in his hands and looked at me with immense love in his eyes, our smiles growing as he leaned in and kissed me. He kissed me like a man truly in love, a man who was going to treasure his wife and treat her like gold. The tears streamed down my face as I realized it was going to be me—I was going to be his wife. He was going to be the best husband ever to a lucky lady—and that lucky lady was me. He leaned his forehead against mine and gently wiped away my tears, stroking my cheeks with his thumbs.

He straightened up and softly smiled at me. "I have something else to ask you too."

"Okay," I said as we sat back down. "But I'm not sure you'll be able to top that."

He reached across the table for my hands, but I didn't realize it at first. I was too distracted—mesmerized by the ring happily glistening on my finger. This was my first time really looking at it on my hand—and it was magnificent. A double halo of small diamonds surrounded the central cushion-cut diamond, with more small diamonds forming an infinity pattern along the shank. I tilted my hand back and forth, watching as the lustrous gemstones danced in the romance of the fairy lights. Remembering why it was on my finger, I looked at my fiancé to see his face shining as brightly as my new ring.

"I'm sorry." I reached across the table and intertwined our fingers. "You wanted to ask me something else."

"It's okay," he said, smiling as he looked down at the ring sparkling on my finger. "I was hoping you would like it."

"I love it," I whispered, rubbing my thumbs against his hands.

"So, onto my other question." He looked back up at me. "You know how you love my apartment? You said you felt like you belonged there ever since you first stepped inside?"

I nodded.

"What do you think about moving in with me?"

I leaped out of my chair and wrapped my arms around him, practically knocking his chair over.

"So, I'll take that as a yes?" he laughed.

I let him go and smoothed my hands over his shirt, gently tugging it back down from his neck where it got all bunched up between us.

"Yes!!" I exclaimed, returning to my seat, trying to calm my excitement—but not really succeeding.

"It's okay Sunny," he said, still laughing at my uncontrollable cheerfulness. "I've loved your constant enthusiasm since day one. It's one of the things I love most about you."

"Well, you just proposed to me and asked me to move in with you—all within about ten minutes. Of course, I'm going to be excited!"

He reached across the table and took my hands in his. "I am beyond thrilled that we're getting married and you're moving in with me, Sunny. I know we'll wait at least a little while to get married, but you can start moving into my place as soon as you'd like. I'm ready for my home to become our home officially."

We shared a long, silent moment, smiling contently at the exciting new advancements in our relationship. Then I followed his eyes as they moved down and settled on the box in front of me.

"I'm guessing this was your sister's work?" I said playfully.

"When I told her I wanted to ask you to marry me this way, she insisted that she make the cake—so it would be edible," he said with a laugh. "And even though you can read my messy handwriting, you deserve to have it look as beautiful as you." He quietly smiled at me for a moment, then added, "And you really do look beautiful tonight, Sunny."

A SUNNY DAY IN WINTER

"Thanks, Brayden." My heart swelled with love as I looked at my sweet fiancé sitting across from me. Then I thought back to April's constant smiles—starting as soon as I opened my door, then sitting on my bed as she held up the dress, and again during the ride here. "So she knew this was going to happen the whole time? The story about the girl's night out...suggesting that I wear this dress...and then getting me into the bakery without me knowing why?" I shook my head. "She never let on to what was really happening tonight."

"Just like she's always put her complete trust in me, I know I can always count on her as well. We truly do make the best team." He picked up my hand and kissed it. "Make that second-best team."

He got up and went into the kitchen, returning a moment later with plates, forks, and a knife.

"Do we want to cut the cake together?" he asked with a playful smile. "Give ourselves a little practice before we do it for real?"

After taking a picture of our beautiful cake, I wrapped my hand around his, and we cut into it together. We enjoyed our chocolate cake with chocolate frosting, my heart fluttering with happiness every time I looked at Brayden's handsome face glowing in the intimate candlelight. The next time I see her, I'll have to thank my future sister-in-law for all her help in making tonight happen. But right now, I want to focus all my attention on my new fiancé and the romantic moment we're sharing, just the two of us.

Chapter 19

♥

BRAYDEN AND I WASTED no time sharing our good news with everyone. My parents and Lauren were ecstatic to hear about our engagement, and I already have Allison lined up to be my Maid Of Honor. Cassidy is over the moon to be our Flower Girl, but Kyle was a little nervous when we asked him to walk down the aisle with our rings—knowing that all eyes would be on him. He felt better, though, when Brayden told him that he believes in him—which seemed to work just as well on our shy boy as it does on his mom.

We also wasted no time moving in together. We quickly packed my belongings—which wasn't that much. My apartment came fully furnished—an absolute godsend as I started my life over from scratch after my divorce. Besides, everything April picked out fit beautifully in our home, and I felt no need to redecorate.

Ellie moved in the day after our engagement, and when I opened the door to bring her in, a surprise was waiting for us. April and the kids were in the living room, and Cassidy took extraordinary care to ensure her new furry friend adjusted to her surroundings. They had picked up a few toys for her as a housewarming gift, and after a bit of coaxing, the kids played with her while we unpacked the first few boxes.

Every so often, my boss is generous and gives me a weekend day off—just because. Today was one of those rare Saturdays that I wasn't at the spa, and the two of us were at home, unpacking the last of my things—when our attention was pulled to a noise coming from an empty box.

Brayden went over to investigate, laughing when he realized the sound. "It looks like somebody's made herself right at home."

I walked over to see Ellie curled up, sound asleep in a tight little ball, snoring. "Yeah, boxes are her favorite," I said, my laughter matching his. "Your family was so generous to get her some toys—but I think she's gotten more use out of all the boxes. Sometimes before they were even unpacked."

He wrapped his arms around me, letting out a content sigh. "I'm so happy you're here with me, Sunny. It feels great to be making this our home."

"Thanks for asking me to move in with you, Brayden"—I snuggled closer—"it feels like we're a little family setting up our cozy nest together."

A message beeped in on his phone, and he pulled it from his back pocket. He read the text over my shoulder, then said, "Speaking of families, I think mine is up to something."

I stepped back and looked up at him. "What do you mean?"

"'Brayden,'" he read the text out loud. "'We need you at the bakery. The back door is stuck, and you have to come and help us get it open. Love, Mom.'" His face was full of amusement as he looked at me. "Even though I know it's her from the name on display, my mom always ends her texts with 'Love Mom,'" he said, using air quotes. "And somebody else knows she does that too." His eyes twinkled with mischief as he added, "But I'll play along."

He thought for a moment, then stood behind me and put his arms over my shoulders with his phone in front of us so I could watch as he typed his reply:

> Oh, really? The door is stuck, and you need my help?

He sent it, and a moment later, the bubble indicating she was typing a response appeared.

> Yes, and make sure you come in the front door. Sam has been working on it for a little while, and he has a lot of tools in the way.

"This just gets better and better," he said with a laugh.

A SUNNY DAY IN WINTER

I thought of the perfect comeback, so I looked back at him; my eyes lit up with excitement. "Can I type the reply?"

"Go for it," he said, giving me his phone and resting his chin on my shoulder as I typed our response.

> And let me guess, I need to shave and dress nicely to work on this door that desperately needs my attention?

"Good one!" he said, wrapping his arms tighter around my shoulders.

A moment later, we had our answer.

> Of course! We can't have you looking sloppy while you're playing handyman!

Then the bubbles appeared again for another message.

> And don't forget Sunny!

"Like I ever would." He kissed me on the side of my head, then took back his phone for one last message.

> We'll see you soon, April ;)

I turned around to look at him, both shaking our heads and laughing.

"I guess I'll get in the shower while you shave," I said, reaching up and rubbing my thumbs on his handsome but scratchy face.

"Sounds good," he replied with a kiss. "I can't wait to see what these two have up their sleeve this time."

A SHORT BIT LATER, we were out the door—Brayden freshly-shaven and dressed in a blue polo shirt and khakis and me in a light-yellow sundress. We pulled up along The Green and walked hand-in-hand toward the front door, just as instructed. We glanced at each other sideways as we approached, noticing that all the lights were off inside. He grinned at me as he pulled out his keys, put them in the lock, and turned it. The lights came on as soon as he opened the door, and several people jumped up from where they had been crouching behind the tables.

"Surprise!"

Our families were in the bakery with party hats and noisemakers, and you would have thought it was New Year's Eve. A *Congratulations* banner hung against the front wall above the chalkboards, and streamers swayed from the ceiling. Brayden's family and Marissa were there with my parents—and my eyes lit up even brighter when I saw that two additional people had joined the fun. My sister-in-law Katie was in a light purple dress that looked beautiful against her long, dirty-blonde hair, her blue eyes sparkling with excitement. Next to her stood Russ in khakis and a black button-down shirt, his short brown hair and brown eyes contrasting with his wife's much lighter features. He had a small, forced smile on his face, clearly uncomfortable being around so many unfamiliar people. Even though he looked like he wanted to crawl under a table and hide, I was excited to have everyone in the same room.

Cassidy ran up and hugged us excitedly—always the welcoming committee—then pulled us further into the room.

"Thank you for doing this for us," I said as we looked around wide-eyed, taking in all the beautiful decorations.

"Yeah, this place looks great," Brayden added, his eyes landing on his mom and sister, a huge grin spreading across his face. "But I should probably go check on the back door—right?"

April put her arm around Lauren's shoulders, a satisfied smile on her face. "Our master plan worked again."

"We knew you two were up to something. And as transparent as it was, your little scheme was even more fun this time." His eyes brightened as he looked at me. "Because now I have someone special who will play along with me."

We made the rounds and hugged everyone, thanking them for such a thoughtful and wonderful surprise. The ladies had set out a beautiful food display, and we all mingled with our plates full of tasty treats.

Sam assembled a tray of new creations for my dad, and as they sat down together, my dad looked at me with a bright smile. "Hey, Sunny—check us out." They both unbuttoned the top of their shirts, revealing matching donut t-shirts underneath.

"You two are something else," I laughed and shook my head good-naturedly. My laughter calmed to a warm smile as I watched Russ pull out a chair and join them—looking more comfortable to be with just a couple of people now. The warmth in my smile spread to my heart as Kyle discreetly took a seat next to my brother, the two quietly trading one or two-word descriptions about the goodies as they tried them.

April came up next to me, her smile mirroring mine as we watched them together.

"You were right, Sunny. Your brother really is the adult version of Kyle. I don't think Russ said five words the whole time before you got here." We shared a laugh, then she added, "But he and Kyle seem to be hitting it off. I don't know what it is about you two—but my shy, timid son has taken very quickly to both you and your brother."

"I guess there's something about my extreme friendliness and Russ's extreme shyness that makes him feel comfortable with us." I watched them together for another moment before continuing, "And it's nice to see my brother joining in on the fun. Typically, Russ will stand back and watch other people have a good time, too shy to jump in himself—but I guess all it took was a tray full of goodies. It was so nice of Sam to do that for the guys."

Then I turned to her with a grateful smile. "And it was really sweet of you to throw this party for us. And the fun started for Brayden and me at home, playing along with your crafty little scheme to get us here." We shared another laugh, then I took her hand and said, "We were both excited to see what you and your mom were up to, but wow—this party was even more than we expected. Thank you, April."

She pulled me in for a warm hug. "You're welcome, Sunny. We're so happy for you and Brayden, and we wanted to do something special for you two." I noticed a gleam in her eye when she let me go—like she had another surprise up her sleeve.

She walked across the room and said something to Lauren as Brayden approached me and wrapped me in a loving embrace. "Our families are amazing, aren't they?" he said, kissing me on the side of my head.

"They are," I agreed with a smile, looking at his handsome face. "And something tells me your mom and sister aren't done yet."

We watched as April grabbed her mom's hand, and they stepped in front of the counter.

"Can we have everybody's attention, please," April said.

The room quieted as all eyes turned to the two ladies standing in front of us, excited smiles lighting up their faces.

"Thank you for coming to Sunny and Brayden's party; it's so wonderful to have everyone here to celebrate our happy couple." Everybody clapped and cheered for us, then she continued, "But the party is only half of the surprise."

I looked at Brayden to see if he knew what was happening, but he just shrugged and shook his head—clearly as in the dark as I was.

"So, as everyone knows, all of us have a sandwich named after us," Lauren took over. "We had always hoped there would eventually be another name added to the menu board—we just needed to wait patiently for Brayden to add another member to our family." She looked fondly at the two of us standing together, holding hands. "And we are so happy it's you, Sunny."

The two ladies stepped behind the counter to stand on either side of the chalkboard listing the sandwiches—which I just now realized was entirely blocked by decorations.

April turned to me with bright eyes and a huge smile and said, "Welcome to the family, Sunny. You're officially one of us now!" Then she and Lauren pulled down the glittery streamers to reveal their other surprise.

My jaw dropped, and I grabbed Brayden's hand with both of mine, overcome with joy as I read the updated menu board. Written very delicately in light pink chalk under *The Brayden* were the words:

The Sunny: Fluffernutter on White - Cut on a Diagonal

I looked from the sign to my fiancé, my mouth still gaping open. His eyes sparkled as he looked at me, undoubtedly as happy as I was at seeing my name added to the menu board. Then my focus shifted to Lauren and April's smiling faces, love radiating through me as I looked at them. I wasn't even sure what to say—deeply touched by their sweet gesture of inclusion. So I just stepped forward and hugged them, feeling strongly like a part of the family.

Brayden stepped forward and hugged his mom and sister as well, speaking for both of us. "Thanks, Mom. Thanks, April. This means a lot to Sunny and me."

I nodded in agreement, then wrapped my arms around my fiancé as I marveled at the new addition to the menu. I could hardly believe that my name was now officially included in the family business. Brayden pulled back slightly and slid his hand under my chin, tilting my face toward him. As soon as my eyes landed on his bright smile, I knew exactly what he was thinking.

"Let's tell them," I said, my smile growing to match his.

He took my hand and led me back into the middle of the room. "Sunny and I have an announcement of our own."

We stood there and smiled at each other—prolonging the suspense.

"Well?" April demanded impatiently.

"We've set a date!" I clapped my hands together excitedly.

A collective gasp of happiness went around the room. April and Lauren's eyes lit up as they hugged each other, and my mom's did the same as she hugged my dad.

"That was fast," April said, her eyes growing more excited as she looked at us. "You two only got engaged a week and a half ago!"

Brayden slid his arm around my waist, an affectionate smile spreading across his face as he gazed lovingly at me. "I would marry Sunny tomorrow, but she wants a winter wedding. And as long as she's happy—I'm happy."

"Aww," all of the ladies in the room gushed at the same time.

My smile broadened as I looked at my fiancé. I really am the luckiest girl in the world.

"So, when exactly in the winter?" my mom asked.

"The Saturday before the Winter Carnival," I answered. "We've already talked with Danielle and Patrick, and they're thrilled to host our wedding at the Victorian Inn."

Everyone came up and hugged us, offering their congratulations. Our moms started talking excitedly with April, Marissa, and Katie—already sharing thoughts for menu ideas, dress styles, and decorations.

I smiled at Brayden. "This is just what females do."

He smiled and shrugged. "It's all just details to us guys." He brushed my hair over my shoulders, his fingers following the entire length. "And I already know the most important detail of all. You are going to be the most beautiful bride ever." His eyes were sparkling as he leaned in and kissed me, and I knew he was dreaming of me walking down the aisle to him.

"Good news Brayden." A voice across the room pulled us out of our private moment. We looked over to see Marissa with a mischievous smile on her face. "I think someone has finally gotten the hint that you're off the market now."

"That's right," April chimed in, putting her arm around Marissa's shoulders and looking at us. "Vicki stopped by this morning and said to pass along her congratulations to you and Sunny."

Brayden let out a laugh of relief. "Good, I've been waiting years for her to stop hitting on me."

My family all snapped their heads in his direction, their eyes wide with confusion.

I picked up Brayden's hand in mine and turned to them with an explanation. "There's a middle-aged lady in town who's been trying to lure Brayden into her cougar's den for years. I saw her friskiness first-hand—starting at the snowman competition and then again when I returned here a few days later."

Now that it made sense to them, their wide eyes turned to good-natured laughter.

April smiled at me as she pointed to where we sat that day. "Sunny's been saving Brayden from Vicki since she held his hands at that table right over there."

Brayden and I smiled at each other as everyone turned toward the table. Once again, we secretly shared our memory—knowing what truly happened the moment I intertwined my fingers with his.

"And *you* might be off the hook, but she did ask about a guy named Josh," Marissa said.

"How did she find out about him?" Brayden asked, shifting his focus to his sister.

"It was not me," April answered with her hands up in the air. "I swear that woman has radar. But if you want to keep Josh as a friend, you might want to warn him about Vicki before he gets here."

"Good thinking," he agreed with a laugh.

We all continued celebrating for a while, everyone excitedly talking about our upcoming wedding. Brayden and I were standing together near the door, watching our families from afar, when my parents, Russ and Katie, approached us.

"We're going to get heading home now," my mom said, hugging me goodbye. "Congratulations again." She hugged Brayden and said, "It's so sweet how you and your family treat Sunny. We're delighted she found you."

"Brayden"—my dad extended his hand to my fiancé—"this has been a wonderful party. Your family has once again been very hospitable to us."

"I'm glad you had a good time, Rob," he said, shaking my dad's hand. "And I know Sam was happy to see you again."

We laughed as my dad waved to his new best friend across the room, smiling and pointing at their matching t-shirts.

Then Brayden turned to Russ. "And we're happy you and Katie were able to join us. You should stop in more often."

"Okay, thanks," my non-chatty brother managed a two-word reply.

Being the friendlier one, Katie hugged Brayden and me, saying, "We'll make sure to do that. The guys had so much fun taste testing with Sam, and we even made two little friends."

Cassidy must have known she was being talked about because she came running up and hugged everyone—holding onto my brother for a little longer than everyone else.

"Bye, Russ, you're my favorite new friend!"

"Bye, Cassidy," he said with a shy smile, patting her on the back.

"Bye, Kyle," my mom said gently to the timid boy standing a few feet away.

"Bye," he said quietly. He stood there for a moment, looking at everyone. Then he slowly stepped forward to hug only one person—my brother.

"Birds of a feather," I said to my mom, smiling fondly as she watched them.

I hugged everybody one last time, and then my family headed out the door.

"Today was such a great day," Brayden said, wrapping his arms around me. "I love that our families get along so well."

"Me too," I agreed, relaxing in his arms. "And I know they feel just as welcome here as I always have. Your bakery has felt like home to me ever since I walked in the morning of my birthday."

He stroked my cheek as he looked at me, the love shining in his kind, blue eyes. "I'm happy to hear that, Sunny, because I waited a long time to have someone special to share this place with. I know April and I are the owners, but I consider the bakery to be just as much yours as it is mine." He ran his fingers down the length of my hair, his handsome face coming closer to mine. "And I meant what I said earlier—I really would marry you tomorrow. I can't wait until you're walking down the aisle to me. I already know it will be the happiest moment of my life."

I reached up and slid my arms over his shoulders, our smiles meeting as he leaned in and kissed me. I could feel the love circulating through him, the anticipation of me becoming his wife. And honestly, I was just as excited. I can only imagine how handsome he will look standing at the front of the aisle—waiting for me in a tailored suit. Only now, I don't picture him as Mr. Executive. I picture him as my future husband.

Chapter 20

♥

Five Months Later

IT WAS THE MONDAY before our wedding, and we were gathered at April's house for the final pizza and movie night before our big day. Our wedding plans came together quickly over the past five months, with Danielle and Patrick taking care of many of the details. Their excitement to host our big event was apparent right from the start, commenting that they noticed something special between us during the snowman competition.

Having been through this before, I know what's essential with a wedding—and what isn't. We decided that all the expensive fluff didn't matter, wanting to keep it small and intimate—focusing on our love, not grand rituals or traditions.

Much to everyone's surprise, I only tried on one wedding dress. Allison came as her always prepared self—complete with water and snacks—expecting a long day of indecision. But as soon as I put it on, I knew instantly—just like when I met Brayden—that it was the one for me. An elegant, beautifully simple, sleeveless ivory gown that will pair perfectly with a delicate shawl to keep my shoulders and arms warm.

We decided—or rather, I had decided since Brayden had no clue this was a thing—on purple and turquoise for our wedding colors. Allison picked out a beautiful plum-colored gown for herself, and we had a friend make a cute, sparkly turquoise dress for Cassidy. The only wedding attire I haven't seen yet is Brayden's since we both want to be surprised when we see each other at opposite ends of the aisle.

I've decided not to do three typical bridal traditions—opting only for *Something Old*. Right before I left for my first military deployment, my grandmother gave me a small rosary given to her as a child. It came with me on both deployments—a comforting reminder of home. It will be tied around the stems of a simple bouquet of pink tulips—the only flowers I need.

I officially left massage therapy in September to work exclusively at the bakery. *The Sunny* has been a big hit with the lunch crowd, nostalgic smiles spreading across happy faces as they reminisce about their childhoods.

In October, we celebrated Brayden's thirty-fourth birthday by going to New York City, just the two of us, so I could see where he used to work and meet his friend Josh. When we returned home, we celebrated with his family and our favorite fall time traditions—apple picking and getting lost in a corn maze. We enjoyed our first holiday season together, with our apartment looking so festive—complete with a tree and three stockings since we included gifts for Ellie. We rang in the New Year with a kiss at midnight—the perfect start to the six weeks leading up to our wedding.

We had just finished our pizza, and we were all claiming our bowls of popcorn and sitting down in the living room when April smiled at the two of us and said, "I can't believe this is our final movie night before you two officially become Mr. and Mrs. Brayden Montgomery."

Lauren smiled at us as well, then turned to the family and said, "I think we should let the bride-to-be pick the movie tonight. What do you guys think?"

Everyone agreed, so I answered without hesitation, "Ice Age, the original one." I looked around, smiling at everybody, and added, "For two reasons. First, it's what we watched at my very first movie night almost a year ago."

Everyone's eyes lit up, remembering back to that night.

"And secondly," I continued, my smile growing, "I didn't tell you then, but it's actually my favorite movie."

"Really?" April said, her eyes glowing brightly. "I guess we just happened to pick the right movie then, didn't we?"

I nodded. "And Sid the sloth is my all-time favorite character. He's so funny."

"And you two have the same name," Brayden said playfully as he leaned in to kiss me.

"So, your real name is Sydney?" Lauren asked. She had a thoughtful look on her face as she added, "I guess we never did ask you that."

"It's okay," I said to her with a smile. "Your son asked me the day we met."

April crossed her arms and looked at her brother. "So you've known this whole time and didn't say anything?"

"Yup."

She watched us for a moment, her expression softening as Brayden slid his arm around my waist and pulled me closer to him.

"I guess we never thought to ask since we've always just seen you as the cheerful ray of sunshine that brightened up my brother's life a year ago."

"And you've continued to do so every day since," Brayden whispered in my ear as I stretched my legs out on the couch and leaned back against him.

Sam started the movie as my soon-to-be-husband wrapped his arms tightly around me—Ice Age becoming increasingly special to me every time I watched it.

A FEW HOURS LATER, we were back at our apartment—Brayden standing behind me on our deck, holding me close as we enjoyed the fresh night air. The sky was perfectly clear, the full moon and twinkling stars setting an incredibly romantic atmosphere for a couple about to get married. We silently admired the view for a few minutes, the soft glow of the night sky making our peaceful surroundings look even more serene. Wanting to see my favorite view of all, I turned around and looked up at my fiancé, his smile glowing as his eyes met mine.

"Did you have a good time at movie night?" he asked.

"This was my favorite one yet," I replied, my smile matching his. "Not only did we watch my favorite character from my favorite movie, but this time after watching Ice Age, I'll actually get to kiss you goodnight." I reached up and tugged at the collar of his coat, but right before our faces met, he stopped. He lingered right in front of me, just like that first night in April's driveway, and we both laughed as we remembered back to that moment a year ago. "Poor Sam, he had no clue we were even there."

"April yelled at him for an hour after you left that night." Brayden leaned his forehead against mine as we laughed again. "But it all worked out okay. Our kiss in the kitchen two days later was the best kiss of my life." His smile glowed brighter as he cupped my face in his hands, our lips finally meeting for a long, affectionate kiss.

"That was the best kiss of my life, too," I agreed. "And they've just gotten better and better each time." I slid my arms around his shoulders and kissed him again before I added, "And I know I'll love them even more once we officially become Mr. and Mrs. Brayden Montgomery."

"Me too," he whispered with a gentle smile.

He took my hand and led me through the door, and I waited as he quietly folded our coats and scarves over one of the maple chairs. Then he retook my hand and led me to the loveseat, picking up my legs and draping them across his lap.

He ran his fingers through my hair, tucking it behind my ear, as he looked at me for a long moment, the love shining in his eyes. His hand settled on my legs as he picked up my hands and said, "You are so beautiful Sunny, and I can't wait to make you my wife."

"Thanks, Brayden." I leaned forward and kissed him. "And I can't wait to be able to call you my husband."

"There's something I've been thinking about for a few hours," he said, intertwining our fingers and rubbing his thumbs against mine. "Something that hadn't occurred to me until my sister mentioned it, and then you said the same thing on the deck. I want you to know, Sunny, you're more than welcome to take my name—but don't feel like you have to."

Caught off guard, I wasn't sure what to say at first—not expecting him to bring this up.

"I guess I hadn't really thought about it either," I admitted.

So, I thought about it.

"Well," I began, "I changed my name last time and never really felt like that person. It was like I was expected to take his name, and I felt like I had lost my identity. Once my divorce was final, I changed my name back to Jackson—and it was so…amazing. I felt just like myself again."

"While Sunny Montgomery does have a nice ring to it," he said with a playful smile, "I would never want you to feel like you lost your identity. I love the person that you are, and I always want you to feel like yourself—even if that means not taking my name."

As we sat there talking, I felt my love for this fantastic man flourish immensely. I'm not sure how many men would support their new wife keeping her name—let alone initiate the conversation. I was contemplating various options when a compromise occurred to me.

"There's always hyphenating, I suppose. That way, I can take your name and still keep mine as well."

A smile spread across his face as he thought about it. "So, I guess that would make you Sunny Jackson-Montgomery."

As soon as I heard our names together, I sat up straighter—immediately realizing it was not an option. "I can't do that."

"Why not?" he asked, his tone curious yet supportive.

"Jackson Montgomery?" I said, staring at him wide-eyed.

He just shook his head and raised his eyebrows questioningly.

I laughed and leaned in to kiss him. "I guess being a guy, you wouldn't know this—but Jackson Montgomery was one of Erica Kane's many ex-husbands on the soap opera I grew up watching with my mom."

He laughed and said, "When you put it that way, I will agree with you—hyphenating is certainly not the way to go." His laughter calmed to a sweet smile, and I knew I was looking at a man unfazed by ego or tradition. "So...Sunny Jackson it is?"

"Sunny Jackson it is!" I confirmed with a smile that matched his. I gazed into his loving eyes—still so fascinated that such a wonderful, open-minded man even existed. "A little confession?" I said, rubbing my fingers back and forth against his.

He picked up my hands and kissed them. "What is it, Sunny?"

"When I got divorced, I wasn't sure I would be able to get married again," I said quietly, looking down at our hands lying in my lap. "That first time we were in your dad's workshop together, and I told you that I was open to finding true love—I really did mean it. I was hoping so bad to find a great man, someone to share my life with, but I wasn't sure if I would be able to take that final step. I thought that getting married again would be closing my escape hatch—and that terrified me."

I looked up at him to see the ever-present understanding in his eyes as he listened to me. "But then I met you," I continued, as a smile spread across my face. "And it wasn't long at all until I pictured myself marrying you. And there was no fear, no doubts—just a whole lot of excitement and dreams of a future with you. I guess the biggest reason I didn't think I would get married again was that I was afraid you didn't exist. But here you are. And I'm the lucky girl who gets to walk down the aisle to you in five days." I picked up his hands and gave them a gentle kiss, holding them against my lips for a long moment. "So thank you, Brayden, for making me feel safe enough to trust you with my heart. It's because of the security that I have always felt with you that helped me to believe in marriage again."

He pulled me in for a long hug, and I felt so much love radiating through his embrace. He cupped my face in his hands and said, "Thank you, Sunny, for telling me this. I'm so happy that you trust me with your heart and you feel safe with me. I promise I will be the best husband I can be every day for the rest of our lives."

"I know, Brayden," I said, reaching up and stroking his cheeks with my thumbs. I gazed into his loving eyes, a playful smile tugging at the corners of my mouth as I added, "And even though I'm not changing my name, I can't wait to become Mrs. Brayden Montgomery."

He let out a little laugh. "So, I guess that makes me Mr. Sunny Jackson." His eyes were sparkling with happiness as his face inched toward mine. "And Mr. Serious and Mr. Executive don't hold a candle to that title."

I closed my eyes as his lips met mine, sliding my hands over his shoulders and pulling him closer to me. I said another silent prayer of gratitude to the universe, joy spreading through me—knowing that in just five short days, I would be celebrating the happiest day of my life.

Chapter 21

♥

Resplendent in the early afternoon sun, rays of happiness danced in the parlor of the Victorian Inn. My place on the stairs gave me the perfect vantage point, with the fresh layer of snow outside setting the most romantic backdrop for a winter wedding. Rows of chairs were set up in the middle of the room, our friends and families whispering amongst themselves as they awaited our entrance. I could see almost to the front of the aisle; the only people not visible to me were Brayden, Josh, and our Justice of the Peace. That's okay, though; I wanted to wait to see my handsome groom until I was making my way down the aisle to him.

I smiled as I watched Cassidy standing on the bottom step with a basket of rose petals, hardly able to contain her excitement as she waited for her big moment. Kyle was standing on the step behind her, nervously holding the pillow with our rings—not nearly as excited as his sister. Allison was two steps up from him, looking so beautiful in her plum-colored dress, a silver barrette in her brown hair, and a small bouquet in her hands. My dad and I were standing together right behind her, holding hands as we waited for our cue. I looked down at the tarnished little antique rosary tied around the stems of my pink tulips, a wave of sentiment sweeping through me as I remembered the January day my grandmother gave it to me. My heart was so full of joy as I waited my last few moments on the stairs, feeling like the luckiest bride in the world. Yet again, I prayed a silent word of gratitude to the universe—not a single doubt in my mind that this is precisely where I am meant to be.

I looked up to see Patrick standing at the back of the aisle as our photographer, smiling at me with his thumb in the air. I smiled back and gave him a thumbs up in agreement; then, he nodded to Danielle to start the music. Instead of the traditional wedding march, we would all process down the aisle to the classic *Chapel Of Love*.

Cassidy knew this was her moment to shine as soon as the song started. Even though her back was to me, I knew she was smiling from ear to ear as she walked down the aisle, dropping her rose petals as she went. I could see our guests smiling at her as she walked by each row, and it warmed my heart, knowing that soon she would be my niece officially. When she got to the front of the aisle, she looked in her basket and realized she still had several petals left, so she tipped it over, and they all landed in a pile in front of her. Our guests had a good laugh, and she relished the attention as she took a seat with her parents.

Next up was Kyle, who stood frozen in his spot. Our shy boy already doesn't like the focus on him, and I think seeing the attention his sister received made him even more nervous. I could see April motioning to him to walk toward her, and he turned around to look at Allison, my dad, and me. "It's okay," I said with an encouraging smile. "You'll do great." Then he turned back around and ran down the aisle with our rings, trying to get the spot-light off himself as quickly as possible. His plan backfired, though, since he got plenty of good-natured laughter out of our guests. He jumped into April's lap, and Sam gave him a high five, and I could see both of his parents praising him for a job well done. I got my first glimpse of Josh as he stepped forward and untied our rings from the white satin pillow, then he disappeared again to return to his spot.

Allison was up next, and she turned around and smiled at me, reaching back to squeeze my hand. I returned her smile, then watched as she walked down the aisle, feeling so grateful to have her as my best friend and Maid of Honor. She was a tremendous help with the wedding preparations and did a beautiful job with my hair this morning. She vanished from my line of sight as she got into position to wait for my dad and me.

We were the only two left on the steps, and we turned to each other and smiled.

"Are you ready, Sunny?"

"Definitely!" I replied.

My breath caught in my throat as soon as I stepped off the stairs—my handsome groom now visible as he waited for me at the front of the aisle. Dressed in a flawlessly tailored black suit, with a crisp white shirt and lavender tie, the silver cufflinks at his wrists were shining just as brightly as his smile. His clean-shaven face was beaming, so full of love and joy, as he watched his soon-to-be-wife make her way toward him. I kept my eyes on Brayden as I once again followed the trail of rose petals leading to the man of my dreams, and I thought, *Wow! I am the luckiest girl in the world!*

Everyone was now standing, and all eyes were on me as I approached the rows of guests. Well, most of the eyes were on me. Patrick was standing just behind the chairs, taking pictures of my dad and me as we walked—but his attention was now at the front of the aisle.

"Look at Brayden! Look at his face!" he voiced his admiration as we walked past him.

My dad and I got to the end of the aisle and stopped, laughing a little as we looked down at Cassidy's pile of rose petals. He kissed me on the cheek, and then he went to sit next to my mom in the front row as I handed my flowers to Allison. I turned to face my beaming groom, tears filling my eyes as I looked at him standing before me. He looked even more handsome up close, the happiness radiating from every part of his face.

He reached out and took my hands. "You look so beautiful, Sunny."

"Thank you, Brayden," I whispered. "You look very handsome."

We shared a smile, and then we turned our attention to our Justice of the Peace. A kind lady with short brown hair and silver glasses, her purple and white officiant scarf contrasted beautifully against her black clothes.

"Dearly beloved," she began. "We are gathered here, on a sunny day in winter, to join Sydney Michaela Jackson and Brayden Alexander Montgomery in marriage."

Then we exchanged vows, put on each other's rings, and sealed the deal with a kiss.

"YOU REALLY ARE THE most beautiful bride in the world," Brayden said, reaching across the table and taking my hands in his. I loved how his hand looked wearing his wedding ring—the baguette diamonds sparkling in the mid-afternoon sunshine streaming through the bay window.

"Thanks, Brayden," I said, smiling at him. "And I'm not the only one who looks stunning in black. My husband always looks so handsome in his tailored suits, but this is my favorite one so far." A feeling of joy spread through me, loving how it sounded to call him 'my husband.'

We turned to look at our guests enjoying their meals in the beautifully decorated dining room. Scattered snowflake confetti shimmered against the white tablecloths—the subtle embellishments blending harmoniously with the bright purple napkins and turquoise vases containing various flower arrangements. Yellow birch place card holders in the shape of snowflakes—handcrafted by the groom himself—sparkled with cheer as the sun caught the coating of glitter paint. Little snowman cards displayed our guests' names in April's exquisite handwriting. Between the sparkling decorations inside, and the sun reflecting off the fresh snow outside, it felt like a magical winter wonderland.

The inn had prepared a sweetheart table in the front of the room for the two of us—complete with a vase for my bouquet and two small candles on either side. Our little table gave us just enough privacy to feel intimate while providing us with the perfect viewpoint to see everyone having fun and getting to know one another.

Josh, Allison, and Nick joined Brayden's family at the table before us, with my family seated right next to them. I smiled as I looked at my grandfather sitting next to my dad. As my only remaining grandparent, it felt very special for me to have him here. The rest of the tables were set up behind them, with the remainder of our guests chatting and enjoying the delicious food the inn's staff had prepared.

After all the plates had been cleared, Josh stood up and clinked a spoon against his glass to get everyone's attention. Dressed in a light gray suit with a white shirt and turquoise tie, his sandy brown hair was combed neatly to one side, and his hazel eyes shined brightly as he looked at us. Until now, Brayden and I had been sitting across from each other, and he stood up and moved his chair to the side of our table. Then he came around to help me with mine, so we were now facing our guests. We took each other's hands and shared a smile; then, we turned our attention to the man standing in front of us.

"For those of you who don't know me, I'm Josh—Brayden's Best Man. I met Brayden seven years ago when we were both starting our first day at a new company. I remember how the two of us thought we were such big shots—finally landing jobs at the most prestigious investment firm on Wall Street. Management, however, had a much different opinion of us—which we quickly learned when they had an assistant show us to our office. Inside, we found two desks crammed into what was basically a closet, no windows, and the only other way it could have felt more like a jail cell would be if she had locked us in after shutting the door behind her." He stopped talking for a few moments as our guests laughed. I looked at Brayden, who was laughing and shaking his head, remembering that day.

"It's a good thing we got along so well," Josh continued, "because we spent three years together in that tiny office. Brayden worked circles around me the entire time, so it was no surprise when upper management offered him the promotion we had both dreamed of since day one." He had been looking around the room at our guests as he spoke, but then he turned to Brayden and said, "Man, I was so jealous when you took me to see the office they were going to give you—it had windows and everything!" I could tell our guests were enjoying his speech because they were laughing and smiling as he spoke. "But then you turned it down, saying you were moving back to Vermont to open a bakery with your sister. At first, I thought you were crazy, but the truth is, I knew I was going to miss my friend—whether you were just one floor up or three and a half hours away. And now that I've been here and seen the bakery, I know you made the right decision. And I'm really happy for you."

A smile spread across Josh's face as he looked back and forth between the two of us. "When the two of you came to visit me back in the fall, and I saw how happy you were, I felt the same pang of envy as when you showed me that corner office a few years ago. But this time, instead of wishing for a big promotion, I hoped that someday I'd find the woman of my dreams. Someone who will make me just as happy as I know Sunny makes you. And that, my friend, is worth more than any fancy job title or the perks that come with it." He raised his glass. "To Brayden and Sunny!"

"To Brayden and Sunny!" everyone echoed.

Brayden got up to thank Josh, and it was nice to see my new husband and his friend laughing and reminiscing about their time together in New York. After a minute, he returned and sat down, putting his arm around my shoulders.

"That was so sweet of him," I said, smiling at my husband. "It sounds like the two of you had a good time working together."

"Yeah, he certainly made that tiny office much more bearable," he agreed, his eyes glowing with gratitude.

My smile turned playful as I added, "And if he's looking for a special lady in his life, we know someone who's looking for a cub to play with in her cougar's den."

He looked at me wide-eyed, shaking his head, laughter eventually taking over. "We like Josh, remember?"

After we shared a good laugh, we looked back at our guests to see that Allison was standing, smiling as she watched Brayden and me together. "Sunny and I have been best friends since the third grade," she began. "We met on the playground at school, and the first thing she said to me was that she had just gotten a cat named Tiger."

"Some things never change," Brayden said, smiling at me and leaning in for a kiss.

"Yes, Brayden, I heard about that," she sighed. Then she turned to address our guests. "You see, our Sunny has a way of sharing too much information about her cats, and right now, it's a gray tiger-striped cat named Elephant that she's always going on about." She stopped for a moment as our guests were laughing—while I looked at my dad and smiled, thinking back to how she got her name. "And I would always get after her to not scare guys off immediately by talking too much about her cat. But I also knew that when the right man came along, he would embrace all of Sunny's quirkiness, which is something we all love about her."

She turned back to look at us, now talking to Brayden. "So when she told me about your first encounter and how you didn't go running for the hills, I knew you must have seen something special in her. And while I did yell at her for not getting your phone number, I didn't scold her for squeaking at you about Ellie like I normally would have done—I just hugged her and told her I was happy for her. And when I met you, I knew you were the man for her. Sunny has been my best friend for twenty-four years, but the truth is, we're more than just friends. Since we grew up with brothers, we became the sisters we each wanted. And in the twenty-four years I've known her, this past year has been the happiest she has ever been. And it's all because of you."

Then she shifted her focus to me. "I felt so bad at the time for having to cancel on you a year ago, but now I see it as fate stepping in. We had been planning our fun day at the Winter Carnival for weeks, and in the blink of an eye, all of those plans disappeared. The universe had bigger plans in store for you, and I feel so honored that you chose me to stand beside you on your big day." She raised her glass and said, "To our newlyweds!"

"To our newlyweds!" everyone repeated, raising their glasses.

I got up and went over to hug her, genuinely touched by her words. "Thank you, Allison. Both for the beautiful speech and for yelling at me a year ago when I told you I was going to stay home and watch tv with Ellie on my birthday." We shared a laugh as we remembered back to her very direct orders that morning. "And I'm so grateful that you encouraged me to go to the bakery by myself to have my cake. Because I ended up getting the best birthday gift of all—I met the man of my dreams." Gratitude spread through me as I hugged her one more time, then I returned to my table and kissed my new husband as I sat beside him.

"We have some amazing friends, don't we?" he said as he put his arm around my shoulders, and we both looked at Josh and Allison.

"Yes, we do," I agreed, resting my head on his shoulder for a second. Then I turned my attention back to my favorite blue eyes, and just as I got lost in them, we heard another voice.

"I have something I would like to say."

Chapter 22

♥

We turned to see Lauren standing in front of her table, looking at the two of us. She wasn't saying anything, clearly too emotional to speak. April reached up and took her mom's hand, which seemed to help.

"I'm sorry," she began. "I didn't realize I was going to get this emotional before I even started."

"It's okay, Mom," Brayden said to her reassuringly. He took my hand in his, and I looked at him to see that he was smiling at me—as if maybe he knew what she was going to say. He kissed me, and his eyes lingered on mine for a second before we both turned back to the lady standing before us.

She took a deep breath, then focused her attention on me and said, "Sunny, from the first moment you walked into the bakery, I knew there was something special about you. There was a positivity and a friendliness in you that I had never seen before, and I just knew my son had to meet you. April and I were already working on our plan before we even went over to talk to you. As soon as we found out you were by yourself for the day, we couldn't have been happier and immediately put our plan into action. We knew our best chance of getting Brayden outside was to make up an excuse about the bakery. And it worked."

Her eyes shifted from me to her son, and she continued, "That's really why we made up that story about needing the coffee cups. When you showed up under the tent, I told you that it was to get you away from your computer—but it had nothing to do with your computer. It had everything to do with getting you in front of Sunny. And we were quite proud of our little plan too, and how easily it worked. You didn't even question why we told you to shave and dress nicely."

Brayden and I shared an amused smile, remembering back to that first morning and the crafty text message from his mom and sister. We looked back at Lauren and saw that she and April both had satisfied grins on their faces.

"Our plan was working so well; you looked so handsome as you came walking under the tent. But then something happened that even I wasn't expecting. I noticed it in the first second that you saw Sunny. The two of you stood there, staring at each other, neither one of you moving. I saw something in the way that you looked at her—something I recognized." She stopped for a moment and put her hands over her heart. "It was the way your father always looked at me."

A SUNNY DAY IN WINTER

I looked at Brayden for a moment, and he just smiled at me, picked up my hand that he was holding, and kissed it. Then we returned our attention to Lauren.

"April and I both saw it, and we were so happy that we had already asked Sunny to be on your team for the snowman competition. The two of you were making it so easy for us." She looked down at April, and they shared a laugh, still clearly very proud of their plan.

"When the kids came back afterward and told us you had won, we were so excited for the four of you. But then Sam said something that made us happy for just the two of you. Actually, it was two things." She was looking at Brayden now. "First, he told us that he had been watching you while you were building the snowman, and it looked like you were actually having some fun for once. And it wasn't just because you had finally taken some well-deserved time away from work—but you were especially enjoying who you were spending that time with. He said you gave the kids instructions and then worked on your part of the snowman with Sunny. A little team within a team."

I turned to my husband to see him looking at me with a playful smile on his face. "I told you I liked the partner I was working with. I guess Sam saw it too." He gave me another kiss, and then we turned our attention back to Lauren.

Now her focus was on me. "And secondly, he told us about the pictures he took of the four of you after you won the competition. He said he had just taken what he thought was going to be the last picture—but then something happened, and he wanted to make sure you saw it. Brayden was no longer looking at him—instead, his focus was on you. And Sam said that was the happiest he had ever seen him."

This time, the playful smile was on my face as we turned to each other. "Sam took a picture of me smiling at you?" Brayden asked me, wide-eyed.

I nodded. "I saw it when I got home that night. I showed it to Allison and Nick the next day, and that's when they told me to get back to the bakery. Nick said that a man doesn't smile at just any woman like that, and they knew you would want to see me again. The look on your face told them everything they needed to know."

We turned to see Allison, Nick, and Sam smiling as they looked at us. I blew them a kiss of gratitude, so thankful for the roles that all three of them played regarding that one picture—the perfect moment frozen in time.

"And my day just kept getting better the more I discovered about you two," Lauren continued. "When April suddenly told us we had to get in the car and leave Mr. Beauchamp's farm, I thought she was acting like a crazy person. And then I thought she had really gone off the deep end when she told us she had to stop by the bakery, and you had to go in with her, Sunny. The look on your face was priceless as you sat there, just as confused as the rest of us. We all knew to just go along with April when she gets like that, but it was your first experience with Miss Bossy Pants in full swing." She paused for a second as everyone in the room had a good laugh. "But when she got back in the car and told us about the sweet birthday surprise Brayden had set up for you, I couldn't have been prouder of my son. I was wondering why he had pulled his sister aside when he got back up to the top of the hill, and when I found out what he wanted to do for you, my heart just melted." She turned to our guests and said, "My typically unemotional son had planned out a romantic evening with candles, rose petals, chocolate cake with chocolate frosting, and..." She drew out the last part for dramatic effect. "Peanut butter with raspberry jam sandwiches." Everyone laughed again as Brayden and I turned to each other to share another kiss.

"That really was the best birthday of my life," I said with a huge smile.

"It was my pleasure," he said in his deep, sexy voice, his smile growing to mirror mine.

"And as great as that first day with you was, Sunny, it kept getting better as time went on," Lauren continued. "You returned to the bakery two days later and joined us for our Monday night tradition of pizza and a movie at April's. And we were so thrilled to have you there, especially since Brayden actually watched the movie and didn't just work the whole time." She smiled affectionately at us while she paused for more good-natured laughter from our guests. "But then our lives changed forever the next time we saw you."

Brayden slid his arm around my shoulders, and I shifted my focus to him, noticing a sparkle in his eyes.

When I looked back at Lauren, her eyes stayed locked on mine as she said, "Sunny, I knew, without a shadow of a doubt, just four days after I met you, that my son was going to marry you."

A collective gasp of surprise went around the room, and I could hear our guests murmuring to each other. I looked at my new husband, my eyes huge with astonishment at what I had just heard. All I could do was stare at him, just like when we first met. He simply smiled at me and pulled me in for a gentle kiss. After a moment, I turned back to look at everyone in front of me, to see they were all smiling and shaking their heads in disbelief. The only people who were not stunned by this revelation were April and Sam; they had the same calm smiles on their faces as Brayden. I looked back at Lauren, who had been watching me the whole time. She gave everyone a minute to process what she had just said, then she turned to face our guests and began speaking again.

"For those of you who did not get to meet my husband Alex, you should know that he had quite the passion for woodworking. The whole time our kids were growing up, April and I would be in the kitchen baking while the guys were out in his workshop. I always knew how much Alex loved spending time with Brayden, working together on various projects. He was so happy that his son took a genuine interest in his favorite hobby, always eager to learn something new. And I could see that Brayden enjoyed being in his father's shop, working alongside him, but it took me years to realize just how much their time spent together really meant to him. It wasn't until my husband died that I truly grasped how much our son loved being in there with him.

"And I didn't fully understand how much the workshop itself meant to Brayden until about two and a half years ago. He never wanted anyone else in there with him after his father died; he said it was their special place, and no one else belonged there. One day, April and Sam stopped by, and he noticed that my kitchen sink was leaking, so I told him he could find a wrench in one of Alex's toolboxes. Sam hesitated for a moment, figuring that Brayden was probably in there. I told him just to pop in quickly, grab the wrench, and leave—hoping that if he was fast enough, Brayden might not even notice. So he reluctantly headed outside and was back before I knew it. He came into my kitchen empty-handed, shaking his head. When I asked him what happened, he said Brayden had met him at the door and told him to leave, that he didn't want to be disturbed. I had a good mind to go out there myself, but I decided not to, knowing that his father would take care of this for me.

"You see, my husband was a rather easy-going man, but the one thing he was strict about with our kids was that they always treat people with kindness and respect. And if they ever were impolite to anyone, he expected them to apologize and make amends right away. Sure enough, a couple of minutes later, Brayden appeared in my kitchen with a wrench and an apology for his brother-in-law."

She turned back to face us, now looking directly at Brayden. "You turned to leave, and I grabbed you by the back of your shirt and spun you around to face me, and I said, 'Brayden Alexander Montgomery.'" She turned around and said to our guests, "He knew right then and there that Mom meant business." The other moms smiled and nodded in agreement. Then she turned back to face her son again. "I said, 'Brayden Alexander Montgomery, are you ever going to allow anyone to come into your father's workshop?' And I will never forget that look on your face as you put your hands on my shoulders, looked me square in the eyes, and said, 'Mom, I promise you, when I meet the woman I'm going to marry, I will bring her to Dad's workshop so she can meet him.'"

My jaw dropped, and I turned to look at Brayden, who smiled gently at me as he ran his fingers through my hair. My eyes filled with tears as all of my memories from that day came flooding back to me—starting with our kiss in the kitchen. The emotion that I felt in his kiss and saw in his eyes as he told me he needed to bring me somewhere. Then standing in his mom's driveway, my hands tucked inside his coat, feeling his heart pounding. The way he led me out back and stood in front of the barn door—the heaviness hanging in the air until he stepped forward to slide it open. And then actually being inside his dad's workshop and finding out I was the only one he let in there—telling me he knew I belonged there as soon as he kissed me. The whole time, I felt like there was some major significance to him bringing me there—but I had no clue that it was something as momentous as this.

But his family knew. My mind flashed to the look on their faces as they each walked in on us, all of them stunned to see me there. I was so confused at the time, but now it all made sense. They knew exactly what it meant for me to be standing there next to him. I remembered how I felt after they left, standing in Brayden's arms after he downplayed their reactions—figuring that all would be revealed to me when the time was right. No one said anything for a year—waiting for the perfect moment. And the moment couldn't have been more perfect.

I looked out at our guests, and there wasn't a dry eye in the room—they were all so touched by what Lauren had said. My eyes passed from April to Sam and then to Lauren—all three of them had huge smiles on their faces as they watched me. I had officially been let in on the family secret. The secret that I thought had something to do with me...turned out to have everything to do with me. And only me.

I turned back to look at my new husband, tears now streaming down my face. He gently wiped them away, then picked up my hands and held them against his chest. "I told you in the bakery's kitchen that I wanted to kiss you as soon as I first saw you—but I didn't tell you why. Even though I found you incredibly beautiful, it was actually because of some fatherly wisdom my dad shared with me years ago. He told me that when you meet the woman you are meant to be with, you will know it as soon as you kiss her. There will be a special way in which you kiss only her, and she will return your feelings to you through that kiss. In that first instant I saw you, there was something in your eyes that told me you were the woman for me. That's why I couldn't move—I couldn't speak. I remembered what my dad had said, and I knew that kissing you would confirm everything I hoped I was seeing in your eyes. And when we finally got our moment in the kitchen four days later"—he shook his head with astonishment—"wow, Sunny, was it there! And it was even better than how I had imagined it. As soon as my lips touched yours—I knew. And the way you kissed me back, I knew you felt it too. I couldn't believe the woman I had waited my whole life to meet was finally in my arms, returning my feelings. And I knew at that moment what I needed to do. I knew I had to bring you to my dad's workshop. And I knew what bringing you there meant." He let go of my hands and gently cupped my face. He had such love in his eyes as he looked at me and said, "And from that first moment in the kitchen, I have been imagining how you would look on our wedding day. And again—wow, Sunny! You're even more beautiful than I had dreamed."

I reached up and took his hands, holding them close to me. "It all makes sense now, Brayden. I knew I felt something between us that first morning, and I was hoping so bad you felt it too. And I knew I felt something when you kissed me—I knew something was happening. There was such emotion flowing through your kiss—but I didn't realize you knew right then that you were going to marry me."

I paused for a second to smile and gaze lovingly into his eyes. "When I was walking down the aisle to you, your face was so happy, so radiant. And I wasn't the only one who noticed it. You probably didn't hear him, but Patrick was watching you, and he said, 'Look at Brayden! Look at his face!'" I turned and smiled gratefully at Patrick—who acknowledged me with a kind smile. Then I returned my focus to my new husband and kissed his handsome face. "To hear him say that made my heart melt. This day isn't just about me—and hearing someone acknowledge *you* during a moment that everyone thinks is all about the bride...that was my favorite part of our quick little ceremony."

We shared a laugh as he said, "Yes, our wedding will go down as the quickest in human history." Our laughter calmed as Brayden ran his hand through my hair and smiled softly at me. "That look on my face was all because of you, Sunny. As soon I saw you walking down the aisle to me, everyone else in the room disappeared—and all I saw was you. In that moment, I felt like the luckiest man alive. Allison was right when she said that the universe had bigger plans for you a year ago. But the truth is, it had people working behind the scenes for both of us"—he clutched my hands to his chest—"and I don't know what I did, Sunny, to make the universe smile on me and bring you into my life—but whatever it was, I am so grateful that I did it. Because you are the best thing that has ever happened to me."

"I feel the same way, Brayden," I whispered as I held his hands tighter.

We turned our attention to our guests and saw Lauren still standing—tears running down her face. She wiped them away and said, "Sunny, when I walked into Alex's workshop a year ago and saw you there with Brayden—I swear my heart stopped for a second. Seeing the two of you together instantly took me back to my kitchen that morning with Brayden standing in front of me—but this time, there was one major difference. When we were standing in my kitchen two and a half years ago, the look on his face was the most serious I had ever seen him. But when I saw you two in Alex's workshop that night, he looked totally different. He was standing behind you, his arms around your waist, his chin resting on your shoulder, and there was such a calmness in his eyes—a relief that he had finally found you. At that moment, my entire view of you changed, as I knew without a doubt who was really standing in front of me. I went from seeing you as the friendly ray of sunshine who walked into our family bakery just a few days before—to thinking of you as my daughter-in-law, knowing that we would someday be here."

Brayden and I both got up and went over to hug her. My heart was so full of love as I stood in her arms, still processing everything she had said. When she let me go, I took her hands in mine. Knowing there was no way I could top anything she had said to me, I just said what was in my heart.

"Lauren, that was so beautiful." I hugged her again. "All of it." I looked at my mother-in-law with an even more profound affection for her now. "Thank you. You don't know how special I feel and how much all of this means to me."

She smiled gently at me. "Thank *you*, Sunny. For the past year, I have watched the two of you together, and my love for you has grown deeper every day. All any mother wants is for her kids to be happy—and seeing how happy you make my son...I can't thank you enough."

She shifted her focus to Brayden. "And I know April and I really can't take credit for you and Sunny meeting—that was all your father's doing. I overheard the two of you when you were looking at the picture of him and April as I was tidying up after Sunny's parents left. Your dad was behind all of this, and I know he's here with us today. And he couldn't be happier for you."

I watched as Brayden hugged his mom one more time, and I could see by the look on his face just how grateful he was for both of his parents.

Chapter 23

♥

THE DOOR NEXT TO the Princess Helena room opened, and out stepped Brayden, dressed in jeans and a navy-blue sweater. His suit was draped over his arm, and he looked just as handsome now as he did before he changed. Danielle had let me use the Princess Helena room to change out of my dress and into jeans and a pink sweater, and Allison had come in to help me. Josh was staying in the room next door for the night before he went back to the city and told Brayden he could change in there. The two of them did us one last favor as Josh took Brayden's car keys and suit, and Allison followed him out the door with my dress. They returned a minute later, and we gave them each one last hug and thanked them for being the most outstanding Best Man and Maid of Honor a couple could ask for. Then my new husband took my hand and led me back into the parlor, as our parents, siblings, and their spouses were coming back inside.

A SUNNY DAY IN WINTER

"All of your gifts are in my car; you can pick them up from my house when you're ready," Lauren said as she saw us walking into the room.

"And I have your cake," April said with a glowing smile. She had told Brayden years ago that when he got married, she would make his wedding cake for him—and she did not disappoint. But instead of the traditional wedding cake, we opted for cheesecake instead. And since the top layer of a wedding cake is typically set aside for the happy couple to enjoy on their first anniversary, she said that was one tradition we were not going to miss out on. So she surprised us with a small chocolate cake with chocolate frosting to take home with us—something to look forward to sharing a year from now.

"Thanks, Mom. Thanks, April," Brayden said as we gave everybody one last hug good night.

He slipped his hand in mine, and we all walked outside together, waving at everyone as they left. It was a clear night, and the full moon and starry sky set the perfect romantic mood for the end of a beautiful winter wedding. We lingered next to our car for a minute, enjoying each other's embrace under the stars—this time as a newly married couple.

"Are we ready to head home?" Brayden asked as he leaned down to kiss me. "I can't wait to carry my beautiful bride over the threshold."

"Sounds good to me," I said with a smile.

He opened my door for me, and I got in—happiness spreading through me as I turned around to look at my dress and his suit carefully draped across the backseat. Brayden got in on his side, and I noticed him smiling at me as I turned back around.

He picked up my hand and kissed it. "I know I keep telling you this, but you really were the most beautiful bride a man could ask for."

I leaned across the console and kissed him. "And you were a more handsome groom than any girl could ever dream about. This bride considers herself very lucky."

It was a short drive home, and we were pulling into our driveway before we knew it. Two cars were already parked, as April, Sam, and the kids had followed Lauren to help her with our gifts. All the lights in Lauren's house were on, and it warmed my heart as I watched everyone laughing in the kitchen. My ever-chivalrous new husband came around and opened my door for me, and I smiled at him as I took his hand and stood next to him. It felt great to be home.

We took our time as we made our way around the garage and out back to the barn. It was a relatively mild winter night, and we again took advantage of the romantic night sky. We slowly strolled hand-in-hand, newlyweds enjoying each other's company, the moonlight brightening our path through the snow.

As we were walking, Brayden said, "Your grandfather and I stayed holding hands while you were holding the baby."

"Really?" I breathed with adoration. "Brayden, that's so sweet."

A SUNNY DAY IN WINTER

Pure happiness spread through me as I thought back to the moment he was talking about. We decided to take a photo with our oldest guest: my eighty-five-year-old grandfather, and our youngest guest: my cousin's eighteen-day-old baby. Before my aunt placed him in my arms, we each held one of my grandfather's hands—and knowing that the two of them stayed that way for the picture made it feel even more special. One more moment frozen in our history that I know I will cherish forever.

He picked up my hand and kissed it, and I smiled as I noticed my diamond sparkling in the moonlight. "And as nice as that moment was, yours is my favorite hand to hold."

"Mine too," I agreed, leaning my head on his shoulder.

We rounded the corner of the barn, and Brayden led me up the stairs to the deck. He stopped a few feet in front of the door and wrapped his arms around me, wanting to enjoy one final embrace in the moonlight.

After a minute, he let me go and stepped forward to unlock the door. He pushed it open, turned on the lights, then came back over to me. There was such love in his eyes as he smiled at me and picked me up in his arms. He held me there for a moment, giving me one last kiss under the twinkling stars. Then, like the true gentleman he is, he carried me over the threshold and gently set me down in the living room. He was draping our coats and scarves over one of the maple chairs when I noticed something had caught his eye.

"I thought my mom was taking all of our gifts home with her." He turned around to see a huge smile on my face.

I went over and picked up the gift bag sitting on the oak end table he and his dad made when he was in high school.

"She took home all of the gifts from our guests, but this one is from me." I gave him a kiss and handed him the bag.

His face broke into a smile that mirrored mine as soon as he realized what it was. He set the bag down and reached in with both hands, lifting up a frame made of yellow birch—complete with quirky knots and colorful wood grain. The photo inside was of four people standing with a snowman—three faces smiling at the camera, one smiling at me. I stroked his back as we both looked lovingly at the picture, my heart swelling with several fond memories from that day.

"So this is why you wanted me to make this frame for you?"

I nodded. "I had your sister sneak it in here really quick before we got home."

"Thank you, Sunny," he said, leaning down to kiss me.

"You're welcome, Brayden. I knew you would love it—I've just been waiting for the right time to show it to you."

"I can't believe my family knew this whole time and didn't say a word."

He looked at me to see a playful smile on my face. "I guess I had a little inside secret with your family too."

A SUNNY DAY IN WINTER

His eyes were shining with love as he looked back at the picture. "I'm glad they didn't spoil the surprise because this is the best wedding gift ever."

"Over the past year, I've looked at this picture so many times—remembering how I felt when I first saw it on my phone that night. Sam really did capture the perfect moment. You look so happy."

"That's because I knew I was looking at my future wife," he said, running his fingers through my hair.

He set the picture down and cupped my face in his hands. He tilted his head to the side and looked at me the same way he did when he first saw me under the bakery's tent. Then he smiled and leaned in to kiss me in a way that only a man in love with his new wife would kiss a woman. He continued to kiss me as he picked me up in his arms and carried me over one more threshold—the one leading into our bedroom, to start our lives together as husband and wife.

The End

About The Author

♥

Sheri Abild never imagined she would become a writer. Then one day, she decided to write the story she wanted to read. She does most of her writing in one of two places: the pretty pink bedroom in her home that belongs to two cats (with her furry co-author cuddled up next to her snoring), or sitting and looking cutesy in her husband's woodworking shop while he makes a lot of noise. She is the girliest Air Force Veteran who was laughed at by aircrews because of her high-pitched voice. A Vermont native, she grew up an exit down the Interstate from her husband, and they met on a cold yet sunny day in winter.

To stay up to date with her stories and learn neat tidbits about what influences her writing, go to:

www.sheriabild.com